USA *TODAY* BESTSELLING AUTHOR

Dale Mayer

TERKEL'S TEAM SERIES

RICK'S ROAD

BOOK 05

RICK'S ROAD: TERKEL'S TEAM, BOOK 5
Beverly Dale Mayer
Valley Publishing Ltd.

ISBN-13: 978-1-773365-21-3
Print Edition

Books in This Series:

Damon's Deal, Book 1
Wade's War, Book 2
Gage's Goal, Book 3
Calum's Contact, Book 4
Rick's Road, Book 5
Scott's Summit, Book 6
Brody's Beast, Book 7
Terkel's Twist, Book 8
Terkel's Triumph, Book 9

About This Book

Welcome to a brand-new series from *USA Today* best-selling author Dale Mayer, where dark-ops SEALs have special senses and skills, needed to solve intrigue, betrayal, and … murder. A series with all the elements you've come to love, plus so much more, … including psychics!

Stubborn was something Rick had been called a lot. *Independent. A loner.* All true but, once a powerful healer connects to bring him back from the brink of death, Rick is in danger of losing that control and that privacy he so values.

Cara understands Rick's need to be alone, but it's not possible any longer, and that isn't something she's ready to tell him. That and the value of the connection they now share is something he has to find out for himself.

And the sooner, the better, as the attacks on the team continue, their temporary headquarters under surveillance, and their much-vaunted skills nowhere in sight …

Sign up to be notified of all Dale's releases here!
https://geni.us/DaleNews

PROLOGUE

RICK HUCKLEBEE STRUGGLED with his consciousness. Something was here; something was eating at him, and he could feel it.

Danger everywhere.

Somebody was trying to hold him down, and he cried out for help again and again, but he just didn't seem to get any answer. And suddenly there was Terk.

"I'm here, Rick. Calm down. I'm right here."

Rick took several gasping breaths. "Dear God, what the hell is going on?"

"The team was attacked," Terk replied. "You need to rest and recover."

"Am I alive?"

"You are." Then Terk hesitated and added, "You are alive but still unconscious."

At that, Rick stared at the man in front of him. "But I can see you."

"I know you can. You were always good at that."

"Says you," he murmured. "What do you mean, the team was attacked?"

"You heard me. The team, everyone, was attacked, and we all have been struggling to get back to normal. You've been in a coma, part of it self-induced, part of it medically induced, so you could heal. Now we need to carefully bring you back out, but you're fighting everything we're doing."

"Of course I'm fighting everything," he murmured. "I don't understand how any of this could happen."

"None of us do," Terk admitted. "The bottom line is, you're alive, and you'll be with Cara."

"I've felt somebody around me these last few days," he noted, "but the feelings have been getting stronger and stronger."

"Well, people are definitely around you," Terk confirmed. "Have you felt anything dangerous?"

"Yes, that's what I'm trying to tell you." He gripped Terk's hand. "I don't know what it is or who, but, every time I try to move, I can't. It's like being locked up in a prison."

"I know," Terk murmured. "Take it easy, and I'll help bring you back—as soon as it is safe for you. Just give me a little bit of time."

"A little bit of time?" Rick asked. "How much? I need out of here."

"And you're coming out," he replied firmly. "You've trusted me up until now. Don't lose that faith."

"No, no, … of course not." He took several calming breaths. "Just get me up now," he demanded in a hard tone.

At that, Terk smiled. "Open your eyes."

Slowly Rick did as asked, seeing Terk standing here, with Calum beside him.

Rick stared at them for several moments, waiting for his consciousness to slowly filter in. "Jesus. Am I ever glad to see you both."

Cal reached out, obviously caught up in emotions, and gripped his buddy's hand. "The feeling is mutual, man. I'm so damn glad to see that you're awake."

"What the hell happened?" Rick murmured. But his

voice was a croak, sounding nothing like it was supposed to. He tried again. "What happened?"

"Too much." Terk nodded. "At least too much to explain all at once. Listen. We need you to recover slowly and to get back on your feet."

"There's no such thing as recover slowly in my world," he snapped. "You know that."

"You might find things are a little different now." Terk searched Rick's psyche, aura, and expression.

Rick stared at him. "In what way?"

"You may have lost a few abilities," Terk replied, "or you may have gained something. I don't know."

Just then a voice that Rick knew drew closer. "I really think this is a bad idea."

"You might," Terk agreed, "but he's awake, so there's not a whole lot we'll do about it now."

Rick stared at the woman beside Terk. "It's been you." He frowned at her, his tone almost surly. "You're the one who's been looking after me."

She nodded. "I have. Terk hired me."

"I feel like—" And he stopped, shaking his head. "I know it sounds stupid, but I feel like she's involved."

At that, Terk stiffened. "Involved in what?"

"I don't know." Rick studied her.

Terk turned to look at her. "Have you had any other visitors?"

She shook her head. "No, I told you that. We've also got cameras all over the place. We also know that, when they come out of the coma, they're very disoriented." She glared at Rick. "So I don't know what you mean by *involved*, but I'm certainly not involved in anything untoward. I've been here for the last several weeks, looking after you."

Terk reached out a hand and gently patted hers. "And it's appreciated. He'll need to stay here for a few more days, at least, in order to get his head together."

"Like hell." Rick drew back the blankets and tried to sit up. And blinked.

He was in a room, white, with no carpet, some wood flooring, but he was alone. The room was empty. He turned his head around and stared. "Hello," he cried out, and almost instantly the sickroom door opened.

And that same woman walked in, took one look at him, and raced forward. "Lie down," she barked. "Take it easy."

He stared at her in shock. "Where's Terk?" he asked. "I was just talking to him."

She stared at him. "Nobody's here but you and me," she murmured. And then she helped him lie back down again. "Please relax. You've just come out of a coma. You need to rest." She immediately slapped a blood pressure cuff on him and started going over his vitals.

Nothing she did could change the shock in his head. He wasn't alone; he hadn't been alone. Everyone, including her, had been here.

So what the hell just happened?

CHAPTER 1

RICK OPENED HIS eyes yet again, feeling that same strange parallel-universe feeling. He was pretty damn sure he'd had everybody in his room not very long ago, and yet he couldn't remember what the woman's name was, which was also an indicator of where his brain was at. When he mentioned it again, the woman had said it was just the two of them for the last couple weeks. He struggled with that because it was the opposite of how he felt. As he shifted in bed, his wasted muscles groaned and complained at any movement.

Rick muttered to himself, "Get used to it. We'll be back on our feet and damn fast. Whether you complain or not."

At that, the sickroom door opened again, and the same woman walked in. She smiled when she saw him sitting up. "Hey."

"Hi." He hesitated for a moment, then blurted out, "I'm sorry. I don't remember your name."

She nodded, as if that were the most common thing in the world. "My name is Cara."

He asked, "With a *C* or a *K*?"

She laughed. "Does it matter?"

He shrugged. "Maybe not, but it helps me place you in a spot in my head."

"With a *C*," Cara replied.

"Ah. Your mother was a romantic, many times over," he noted, with a wry smile.

"Oh. Interesting." She looked at him for a long moment.

He felt the intensity of her gaze, as it swooped over him. "I'm fine, you know."

"Good. In that case, you'll get up and move around a little bit today, right?"

He nodded. "Of course I will."

She smiled at that. "I like the enthusiasm, but we need to make sure you don't overdo it."

"Overdo it, hell," he snapped. "I'm not staying in bed, and I need to get ahold of Terk."

"You can call him," she offered instantly.

He looked around for a phone and then realized that's not what she meant. He studied her closely. "What do you know about that?"

"Know about what?" Cara asked in a seemingly innocent tone.

But Rick knew a whole lot else was going on here. Almost immediately Terk's voice blasted in his head.

I hired her. Be nice.

Rick groaned, as the telepathic communication caused an intense pain, almost made his body shake. "And that was Terk right there," he muttered.

She laughed. "Yeah, he has a tendency to come in like a sledgehammer, doesn't he?"

At that, he could only look at her, … speechless.

She shrugged. "What? You think you're the only one?"

"No, … I know I'm not the only one."

"Good," she replied, "then it won't do you any good to sit here and to act like you don't know what I'm talking about, when I said you can call him anytime." At that, she chuckled. "I'll go get you a cup of coffee, and then we'll sit down and discuss what you need to do to get your body into better shape." And, just like that, she was gone.

Holding his head, he whispered to Terk, *Turn down the damn volume.*

That's on your side, Terk noted, with amusement. *And, by the way, welcome back.*

Yeah, Rick winced. *Hell of a welcome. Where am I?*

Manchester, for now.

What the hell happened?

Too much, Terk replied in a clipped voice. *Four of you are up and about, but we've still got team members down. You're the fifth to wake up.*

Well, that's good, Rick noted, and then he stopped. *What about the others?*

They're not quite there yet, Terk murmured.

The whole team?

Yep, Terk confirmed, *all attacked, all down. Not one of you back to normal.*

Normal? Rick repeated, with a bitter laugh. *Did you think we were ever normal?*

Nope. None of us are, he agreed in his usual tone, never any deception in his answers. *And that's why we do what we do.* With that, Terk was gone.

Rick shifted, so he was sitting up in bed. It felt weird. His body felt weird; in fact, it felt like his core muscles had taken a holiday. Everything was off-kilter and out of sorts. When Cara returned with a cup of coffee in hand, he smelled it before she ever got to him. "Is there ever a smell," he murmured, as she placed the cup on the table beside him, "that evokes such an amazing response?"

"Yes, fresh bread."

He looked at her, startled.

She grinned. "I do like my fresh bread." And, just like that, she headed for the door.

"I thought we would sit here and discuss some things."

"Yeah, but you'll need coffee first. Let me know when you're ready for a second cup."

He sent a message to Terk. *Who is she, and why did you choose her?*

She's special, Terk came back. *Besides, you've worked with her a time or two before.*

No, I haven't, he replied immediately.

Terk smiled. *Well, let's just say, she's been a big help with this.*

It's not like you to prevaricate, Rick murmured.

It's not like you to need answers, when the answers are right there in front of you.

At that, he froze. *Do you think maybe I'm not remembering everything?*

Like I said, things are a little shaky when you first come back out. It was the same for everyone, Terk murmured. *Take it easy, hold back on the judgment, and see what comes up. Remember. Your initial reactions may or may not be something you can trust just yet.*

That won't go over well, Rick muttered. *Things are already far from normal.*

Of course not, Terk replied immediately, *but it is what it is.*

That was such a Terk comment.

You don't have to be so fatalistic about this.

Were you hurt? Rick asked.

Not nearly so badly as the rest of you. At least I don't think so. He stopped and added, *The pain for me was more knowing the entire team was down, then trying to provide what everyone needed.*

I can't believe I haven't been awake all this time. You'll have to catch me up.

We will, once you're capable of handling that, Terk noted.

Handling what?

There have been a lot of changes on the team, he replied. *Our support group had been under attack too, and we've sustained some losses. As soon as you and Cara determine that you're equipped for this, we will fill you in on a conference call, if nothing else.*

Do the guys know I'm awake?

They're all being told now, Terk confirmed.

And the others?

Everybody is different. They're all coming back slowly. For a while there I was afraid that someone wouldn't.

Do we know what happened?

A well-executed cyberterrorist attack. We have no idea beyond that.

He had to stop and think about that for a moment. *So we were targeted.*

Hell yeah, we were targeted, Terk snapped, a bitter edge to his voice that was impossible to ignore. *We are still being targeted. And where it goes from here, we still don't know.*

Have you tracked anyone down?

All kinds of people, he replied. *We've got a lot to discuss, and it will take you some time to assimilate. I don't want to put either of us through more than we need to, so I'll get back to you later, and we'll go through it all, when your brain is alert and functioning.* And, once again, Terk was gone.

It was a hard thing for Rick to admit that he still needed healing time. But if Terk said this had been the same for everyone, then, hell, maybe it made sense. As he sipped the coffee, he tested out his body, disgusted to find that he was weaker than a baby.

When Cara returned, he looked up at her, nodded. "Thank you for the coffee."

"Ready for a second cup?"

"Always," he replied immediately.

She laughed. "I hear you. Just something about coffee." Then she disappeared and soon returned with a pot.

"Okay. Now that we have my second cup," he began, "what can you tell me about what happened?"

"I can't really tell you much about the originating incident," she replied. "All I can tell you is that Terk contacted me and said that somebody on his team was in trouble."

"Why you?"

"I don't know." She shrugged. "Why you?"

He winced at that. "If I knew that answer, I'd be a much happier camper."

"Well, I presume it's my skill set," she noted. "So, as soon as you are back up and healthy, I can leave."

And, at that, he didn't know what to say. "Leave?"

"Yep, you are in a small apartment—my office, you may call it—all on your own," she explained. "I've been under strict orders to do my best to keep you alive but also to not let anybody know where we are, keeping our location completely hidden. So I'm not exactly sure what kind of problem your team is involved in, but I'll take Terk's word as gospel any day."

"It's just a little shocking to wake up and to find out all this shit has been going on."

"Absolutely," she agreed.

He wished he could remember anything about what had

happened. He studied her, seeing the long classic lines, high forehead, heart-shaped face, and long brunette hair, tied back into a braid. "Are you a nurse?" he asked curiously.

She nodded. "I am. I normally do specialty nursing for long-term care patients. But, when Terk called, I came."

"You must be good friends."

"He knew my brother," she noted quietly.

He looked at her in surprise.

"Maybe your team did too," she added. "I assumed as much when I came running, but it wasn't necessary. Either way, if Terk needed me, then I was here."

He frowned. "Are you sure I've been alone this whole time?"

She gazed at him with a wide-eyed stare. "I'm not sure what you're asking, but I certainly haven't let anybody else into the apartment."

He nodded at that. "Okay. Any chance of getting some food?"

"Now that is a good sign," she noted. "Food is a very necessary component to you getting out of here. You're also not going anywhere without Terk's permission."

At that, he gave her a flat stare.

She smiled. "You can argue with me all you like, but you'll need to take it up with the boss."

He nodded. "Don't worry. I will. When it's time for me to leave, I'll be gone."

"Great. Just don't do it in such a way that you get me in trouble, okay?"

He shook his head and grinned. "Terk would know the difference."

"He would, but it would still make me feel guilty, like I couldn't do my job."

"I'm pretty sure that never happens."

"Not often," she said, with a bright, cheerful smile. "I can see now that you are healing in leaps and bounds. It looks like my job is nearly over."

"And then what?" he asked.

"Not sure." She shrugged. "Maybe I'll head back stateside."

"Is that where you're from?"

"I have distant family in California, but no one close is left." she murmured.

"Well, I'm sure that, after looking after me for all this time, you're more than ready for a holiday."

"You weren't half bad." She laughed. "I mean, you were in a coma most of the time, after all."

"Well, there is that," he muttered, "but I'm guessing this next phase might be rough."

"Depends on how difficult you'll get." She gave him a flat stare.

He just glared right back at her.

She smiled. "Glare all you want. It won't make a whole lot of difference to me."

He nodded. "No, I can see that, but I'm not particularly sure that anything I say will make a difference."

"It will, just maybe not the way you think."

He wasn't sure what to make of that, but she immediately got up. "I'll go see what we have for food."

"Do you do the grocery shopping?"

"Yes, and then somebody delivers it."

He nodded. "Yeah, the government is pretty good on the logistical support end of things."

She looked at him. "My understanding is that the government is not involved." And, with that, she disappeared.

He frowned at that and sent another telepathic call out to Terk, but he wasn't answering. Finally, feeling frustrated, Rick rummaged in the bedside table and found his phone, smiling to see it plugged in and fully charged. Grateful to have that much of his digital world intact he phoned Terk.

When Terk answered, he told Rick, "You're on Speakerphone."

"Great. Who's there?" he barked.

At that, several voices called out.

Some Rick recognized. Wade, Gage, and Damon for sure. "God damn. It's good to hear your voices."

They all replied at once, with words of support.

"Now, what kind of a shitstorm have we got ourselves into?"

"Well, you chose the right term for it," Terk murmured. "We're still not exactly sure what we're really into."

"Yeah, I get that. I sure wish I was there. Send somebody over to get me. I can heal up there as well as I can here."

At that, Terk interrupted with a chuckle. "Not yet. Not until you can get up, walk around, take care of business, and do a full workout, before you can come here."

"Why the hell is that a thing?" he snapped.

"Because," Terk started to reply and then stopped.

"Because why?"

"Well, I would say, because we needed all able-bodied males we could get, but the truth is, we have an awful lot we're looking after here, and we can't really afford to take on more at the moment."

"Ouch," Rick said. "Talk about hitting hard."

"No choice," Terk stated cheerfully. "We're in the midst of a shitstorm, as you know, and it's not likely to get better anytime soon. So we really do need you back on your feet, and we need you here, but we must have you able-bodied and strong first."

Not a whole lot Rick could say to that.

"Don't feel bad, man. We've all been through it," Gage admitted.

"Yeah," Damon added. "Take your time, and don't push too hard."

Rick replied, "Well, I expect to be there within a few days."

"And, if that's the case, you're more than welcome," Terk noted calmly. And hung up on him.

Rick was getting really damn tired of that. On the other hand, he also knew that Terk meant what he'd said, and, if they needed help, he certainly wouldn't compromise their situation by giving them another person to take care of. As long as Rick was here, he supposedly was safe, but safe from what?

Fuming, he managed to get up and to get to the bathroom on his own, just now realizing how many bodily functions he hadn't controlled before. As he studied his sickroom, when he got back in it, he saw all kinds of equipment, then realized that Cara had literally done everything for him, utilizing IVs, catheters, and anything else that was needed.

When she walked into his room a little later, he looked at her sheepishly. "I'm sorry you had to do all that to see to my care all this time. I hadn't realized, until a few minutes ago, just how involved that must have been."

She looked at him in wonder. "I'm not sure what you're talking about, but, as a nurse, it is something I'm quite used to doing."

He nodded slowly. "And I guess that helps."

"What's the matter?" she teased. "Not used to being down and needing medical assistance?"

"No," he snapped. "Not used to being down and out, not used to needing a nurse, not used to needing anything, in fact."

She laughed. "I definitely get the impression that you are one of those strong guys who doesn't ever want to see themselves in anything other than peak form. But, when you're in a coma, medical interventions are the norm," she stated calmly.

He nodded slowly. "I'm just realizing that now."

"I'm glad you were able to go to the bathroom on your own. That's a huge step."

"And food?" he asked hopefully.

"Yep, that's coming too. It will be ready soon."

He wouldn't dwell on the fact that she had been forced to take care of his personal needs. He was grateful that she had the skill to do so because obviously he hadn't been capable, but that still burned him. He didn't know what had gone on before that landed him in a coma for weeks, but he was bound and determined to find out.

When the phone next to him buzzed, he looked down to see a text from Terk.

This is a reminder that you are still in grave danger. No contacting anyone, no letting anybody know what's going on.

He frowned at that but responded in the affirmative and then sent a follow-up. **More explanation is needed.**

The response, when it came, was disappointing. **When you're back up and running.**

He swore at that because he was pretty damn sure that Cara would be the one who made the decision about whether he was *back up and running* or not. When she returned with a sandwich and a bowl of soup, his stomach grumbled loudly.

"Another good sign," she stated automatically.

He nodded. "I am hungry."

"And that's good. Let's see if we can get you eating at the table. Sit down and let me set this up for you."

He pulled himself from his bed and took a few steps to the nearby chair, where he sat down slowly, feeling the weakness in his body. "How long before this fatigue goes away?"

"You just woke up," she reminded him. "The fact that you're even mobile is huge. Don't expect too much out of your body just yet."

"I expect the max," he stated in a hard tone, "and I'm not staying here while we're in danger and all my friends are too."

She nodded. "I get that. I really do, but there's got to be a level of common sense here."

"And you won't let me get away with it if there isn't, right?"

"Absolutely." She handed him the tray. "Hold this." Then she walked over to the corner and pulled out a TV table. She set it up in front of him.

"I could have walked out to the dining room, you know," he added mildly.

"Maybe," she murmured, "but, for this first time eating, let's keep you where I have an eye on you and where you're not too far from the bed."

He would follow along for a bit, but obviously she didn't know that he was generally strong and healthy, and this type of behavior was quite irritating to him. At the same time, she was doing her best and would have to report to Terk, which Rick understood wouldn't be easy for anybody. Soon she had the table set up, with the height adjusted to her satisfaction. "Go ahead."

He nodded, then picked up the spoon and tasted the soup. It tasted fresh, with a deep flavor, and was quite tantalizing. He stared at her. "Did you make this?"

She nodded. "I like to cook."

"Well, I'm definitely happy to reap the benefits," he murmured.

She chuckled. "I don't usually have to cook for anybody else."

He quirked an eyebrow. "I suppose your patients are usually just fed through tubes, huh?"

"Lots of times," she agreed cheerfully. "If I'm lucky, they get out of the coma though."

He frowned. "I guess the alternative is no fun."

"Nope, not for any of us." She gave him a ghost of a smile.

He nodded. "Did I have any physical injuries? Outside of being a little uncoordinated, it doesn't feel like I'm hurt at all."

"A concussion," she replied. "You had a bit of a head injury that has healed nicely since your accident, but what we just don't know is if there's been any damage on the inside."

He opened his mouth and then closed it, before returning his attention to the soup and taking another sip.

Finally she asked, "What is it you're trying to ask but don't want to?"

He hesitated, then looked at her. "Was I checked over by a doctor?" She gave him a flat stare. He shrugged. "Believe me. I trust Terk as much as anybody else in this entire world, but I'm also not a fool, and I know that sometimes we just can't get doctors involved because there's just too much … weirdness going on with us," he said, for lack of a better way to say it.

She nodded. "I believe somebody did do the initial check on everybody."

"Okay, great." He felt a touch of relief at that thought, then he shrugged. "It shouldn't make any difference. I've certainly seen crappy stuff happen, even with doctors involved."

"Doctors are not infallible," she noted immediately.

"No, they sure aren't," he murmured. "What will you do when you're done looking after me? Because obviously I'm awake now and getting much better."

"Are you trying to tell me that I'm fired?" She laughed.

His grin was lopsided at best. "Nope, not at all, but you can bet that I'm bound and determined to work my way back to joining the rest of my team."

"I got that," she noted, with a grin, "and that's good. It also is good to see you eating."

"Did you think I wouldn't be able to?"

"Well, getting food in is one challenge," she explained calmly. "Seeing how your stomach handles it is the next, and, then of course, it's got to come back out again."

"Any reason to consider that there would be a problem anywhere along the line?" he asked cautiously.

"Nope," she replied, "but that doesn't mean there isn't something we don't know about yet."

"Well, let's hope it's all fine. Anything else doesn't sound very appealing."

She broke off into peals of laughter. "Nope, it sure

doesn't, but the bottom line is to ensure that you're as good as you can be, before you head off into the crazy world out there."

There wasn't a whole lot he could say to that either. He got down three-quarters of the soup, then set it off to the side. "If I finish that, I won't have room for the sandwich."

"You've already eaten more than I thought you would anyway," she confirmed.

He gave her a flat stare. "Hey, I told you that I was hungry."

She left the soup on his tray. "I'll leave that there, just in case you change your mind. Who knows? Maybe you won't like the sandwich."

He laughed, took a bite. "It's a sandwich, and, in my world, that means food and sustenance, which go together. I need to get my health back as fast as possible, so I can return to my world."

"Don't be too eager," she murmured.

He shook his head. "All my friends are in danger," he said quietly. "How am I supposed to stay here and rest, knowing that?" She couldn't argue with that, and he was grateful when she didn't even try.

She picked up the empty dishes when he was done and disappeared.

"What am I supposed to do now?" he cried out.

"See how your stomach handles digesting your food. If it comes back up, you let me know."

He stared down at the bed and around him. "It better not come back up," he muttered to nobody in particular. "That is absolutely the last thing I want to imagine right now."

But he was blessed, and everything appeared to stay

down. A few hours later, he still felt pretty decent. He got up and wandered around the small room, feeling confined already. He opened the door and stepped out into the main part of the apartment. He was dressed in a pair of jogging pants and a T-shirt. That was something. As he walked out, he found her at the computer.

She looked up, nodded. "I wondered how long it would take you to emerge."

"Apparently I was being too circumspect though, because I stayed in my room."

"I was hoping you'd have a nap."

"Not happening, at least not right now."

"Got it," she murmured.

He sat down beside her. "I'm feeling good."

"Good," she murmured, studying him. "If you're asking for permission to get out of here, the answer is no."

He glared at her. "You can't keep me here as a prisoner."

She returned his flat stare with one of her own. "I wasn't planning on it, and it's not me who you have to answer to."

He frowned, looked around the room, and called out to Terk, "Wherever the hell you are, I want to leave."

Almost immediately his phone rang. "Good timing," he muttered, casting a sideways look at her, but she ignored him completely. So either she didn't know anything about the extent of the weirdness between all of them on the team or she knew enough to keep her mouth shut about it. Either way, he appreciated the privacy on her part.

As soon as he answered the phone, Terk said. "I understand you're eating."

"Yes, I'm eating, and I'm doing well. It's time to pick me up and to get me back to the land of the living."

"You do remember why you're there, right?"

"Of course I do," he replied in exasperation. "You also know that I won't be of any value sitting here."

"That's not true," Terk argued cautiously.

"You further know I can be of more value," he reworded it, "if I'm there with you guys."

"I get that you want to be here," Terk noted, "but that doesn't mean it's the right answer. Not now."

"How can it be the wrong one, given everything that's going on?"

"First, we have to find out if anybody knows where you are."

At that, he froze. "You think I'm still in danger? But we haven't had any attacks in all the time that I've been here. Why would you think one would come now?"

"Because I've been shielding you," Terk replied.

He stopped. "All this time?" he asked in shock.

"Yeah, all this time, so believe me. I need you back up and running as much as you can be. Then I can stop the energy drain."

"Good Lord. Are the others able to manage without you?"

"No," he admitted, "at least that's what I have to assume, just like with you. I'm not taking that chance."

"How are you managing that? You can't be a mother hen to everybody."

"No, maybe not," he replied, "but you all got hurt on the job, likely because of me. So, believe me. I'm not taking any chances."

"Why do you think it's because of you?"

"Well, because I set up this team for one thing. Plus, I couldn't even save it when they shut us all down."

"I'm not sure we were at the point of saving, but we had

set up plans to check in with each other coming up soon," he replied. "I was hoping we could get clear of the government and set up our own team."

At that, Terk laughed. "Well, it might make you happy to know that's what all of them are talking about now."

"Good. Don't you dare set up something without me."

"Wouldn't dream of it," Terk said, still chuckling.

"How are the others?"

"Everybody here is much better. They've all gone through what you've experienced as well, and hopefully they're at the point where they're holding."

"I'm going stir-crazy here. So how about you fill me in, so I can at least work at wrapping my brain around it?"

"Fine," he replied. "I'm putting you on Speakerphone though." And, with that, Terk proceeded to fill in Rick on some of the headaches that they had been through. By the time that was done, with the help of others chiming in, Rick had been given the gist of it all.

He was stunned. "Good Lord."

"Precisely. So, as you can see, even though you might think that you're safe, we can't be sure, and we must be certain that we get you back here without anybody knowing where you're going."

"Right." He thought about it. "What about Cara here? Is she in trouble?"

"We have to get her out before it comes to that," Terk noted. "So, the patience I'm asking of you is also needed while we arrange for her to be moved somewhere clear."

"Got it. Any chance that they'll try to follow her?"

"There's always a chance," he noted.

"Damn. This is one hell of a FUBAR."

"It is, indeed, and, if I had any answers to give you, I'd

be happy to share them, but I just don't."

"No, I get it," he murmured. "Things are never that simple. Drones, huh?"

"They've appeared prominently several times," he noted.

"Yeah, and they were used in Iran. Remember? Although they have become one of the more recently used weapons."

Terk nodded. "We're still looking into whether anybody from the Iran mission is still alive. I've got Calum building up his strength to do some remote viewing."

"He needs a ground," Rick stated immediately. "You know that was often my job."

"I know it. That's another reason for you to get your shit together."

"Well, getting my shit together isn't as big of a deal as you're trying to make this out to be," Rick argued, "and I'd do a hell of a lot better if I was there with you guys."

"Maybe, let me talk to the rest of the team, and I'll get back to you."

Frustrated, Rick knew he had to let Terk do that because they were a team, and, when the shit hit the fan, you had to trust everybody, not just those you were expected to. Calum was good at remote viewing, but he couldn't get the distance and lock on to a target unless he had a ground, and that's what Rick usually did for all of them. When Rick was there, all of their abilities locked in with so much more power. Thus it made no sense to keep them apart at any time, but maybe that's what this was all about. Protecting the team. Splitting up the team, making sure that nobody could attack all of them at once anymore.

Before their attack, Rick had heard some whining from the government about Terk's team being dangerous and couldn't be left on their own because too much chance of people going off and creating all kinds of trouble for the government. Rick had heard things like that from time to time, but he didn't think the government would have done anything serious about it. When they shut down the program, Rick had been surprised because a group truly thought of as dangerous was something anyone would want to keep an eye on. But instead the government made the decision to just park the whole team, … as if it had never existed.

That kind of thinking was something Rick struggled with because it made no sense to him, but obviously, to the higher-ups involved, it had been their best option. Or at least the best one they thought they had. As Rick sat here, his mind drifting from scenario to scenario, his frustration built.

Finally Cara looked at him, and snapped, "Stop it."

"Stop what?" he asked in bewilderment.

"You're sitting there, going over everything, and yet you don't have enough information, so you're just creating more stress for yourself."

His jaw dropped, as she glared at him irritability. "Plus, you're thinking too damn loud." And, with that, she got up and stormed off into a room he hadn't even tried to enter.

He assumed it was her bedroom, but he wasn't exactly sure. As he looked around, it seemed to be a modest two-bedroom apartment. A small living room, kitchen, and guest bathroom were visible, plus his room, which he assumed was her office. He saw her closed door, which he assumed was a second bedroom. He heard water running, which made him wonder if that bedroom had its own bathroom too.

That arrangement would make it much more convenient for anybody who was looking after him, he supposed. Besides, there would just be problems with a sick or injured person using the usual smaller bedroom in standard two-bedroom apartments, particularly if they also needed space for a helper and equipment to navigate.

He wandered over and sat down at the dining room or kitchen table, whatever you wanted to call it. It wasn't quite big enough to be either, as far as he was concerned, but then he liked bigger spaces. One of the things that he'd been looking at—for when this was all over—was where he wanted to retire and what he wanted to do, but even now it seemed so far-fetched, since there could be no retirement as long as their lives were in danger.

It's funny because the team had talked and joked about it before, but it had always seemed to be a discussion they tabled in the end. They never got a chance to enact even their vacation plans because they'd been attacked. Every time he thought about that, it made him angry, and then he remembered what Cara had said. Thinking too damn loud. Did she mean that seriously? He hesitated and knocked on her door.

"What?" she asked in a grumpy mood.

He almost grinned at that. "Sorry. Do you want to clarify that comment of yours about my thinking too loud?"

She snorted. "Why? You know exactly what I meant."

He looked at her door hopefully. "Well, I'd like to think I know what you meant, but I'm not too sure."

AS SOON AS she opened the door, Cara gave him that same flat stare. "Stop making excuses and pretending that you don't know what's going on. Do you really think Terk would have brought me on board if he thought I was anything other than up for the job?"

He let his breath out slowly. "So, you do understand."

"That you have telepathic abilities? And what was it you said? Something about you being the ground?"

He nodded slowly.

"Well, good for you," she stated. "That's not an easy position."

"In what way?" he asked, looking at her.

"Well, you're the one who's always in the background. You're the one who's always corralling the power but not getting any of the credit."

"I'm not doing it for the credit," he replied.

"Even better," she said, "because credit doesn't come your way."

Something was just so strange about the way she was talking that he wasn't even sure what to say to her.

She laughed. "You're really not getting everything, are you?"

"Obviously not," he noted quietly. "If you have something that you can clarify, I'd appreciate it."

She shrugged. "Not my job."

"You don't have to be so damn cheerful and irritating about it."

She burst out laughing.

"And, if you know so much, how come Terk hasn't recruited you?"

"He tried actually, but I'm a nurse, not whatever you guys are."

He asked her, "Seriously? He tried?"

She nodded. "Do you think it's only a male talent?"

He flushed. "I didn't say that, but I don't really know what to call it."

"That's because you're the ground," she noted, "and probably don't realize just what value you bring to the team."

"I don't look at it like that," he countered, "and I've never felt that I was less than a full member of the team. And, for the record, I know perfectly well how much value I bring."

"Good." She nodded. "In that case, why are you arguing about staying here?"

He glared at her. "Because I know the full value I bring to the team. And sitting here and doing nothing is not utilizing any of my skills."

She tilted her head. "Do you have any skills left?"

"What do you mean?"

"Everybody, according to Terk, was affected in some way. Have you had any inkling if your abilities are even still there?"

He winced. "I sure hope they are, but, no, I don't know."

"Maybe you need to try it out," she suggested.

"Do you even understand what you're asking?"

"Not my problem," she noted, "but you're the one who's stuck here, wanting to go back to work. What is it that you bring to the table now?"

He froze for a moment, as if unable to respond.

"I don't know about you, but I need a cup of tea. Do you want one?"

He followed along because he wasn't sure what he was supposed to do. "Yes, please. That sounds great."

She made him a cup of tea and added milk, the way he liked it. He sat down on the living room couch. "So, what abilities do you have, Cara?"

"I'm not sure I even know," she replied. "I've never bothered to look into it."

He frowned. "You know that Terk has been on the hunt for people like you for a very long time."

"Yeah, he has known about me for a very long time."

"He's a great coach," he added.

"Just because I can do things, it doesn't mean that saving the world is where I belong."

"I'm really surprised to hear that," he murmured.

"I work on an individual level," she explained. "I can save individuals, but I'm not so sure about saving more than that."

At that, he stared at her. "How bad was I?" he asked. "What did you have to do to keep me alive?"

She considered him for a moment. "Let's just say, I don't think you would have made it without help."

He sucked in his breath. "That bad, *huh*?" he asked.

"You were the worst of them, I think. So bad that the news shook Terk to the core."

"Good God. If that were the case, why were your efforts used on me and not the rest of them?"

"Because you were the worst," she stated, "and Terk didn't want to lose you. I think he felt like other people could help the rest of your friends."

He just stared. "Okay," he murmured, "and you're still not telling me how bad it was, why?"

She took a moment and blew out a long exhale. "You were disconnecting. You had no interest in even staying alive anymore, but, worse than that," she murmured, "your cord had started to separate."

He stared at her in shock. "*Started?*"

She nodded. "Started."

"And you could stop it?"

"Well, I did," she admitted. "I wasn't sure I could, and I told Terk that."

"Wow." Rick raised his eyebrows. "You are a person of many talents."

"I am," she agreed, without any guile or argument.

He burst out laughing.

She grinned at him. "It's sure good to hear you laugh."

"Well, you're definitely giving me something to laugh about," he replied. "You are quite an interesting person."

"Yep," she said, "and there are reasons why we do the things we do. In your case, I agreed because Terk called in a favor."

"Must have been a big one."

She sighed. "Honestly I probably would have helped him anyway because it is what I do."

"So you help people who are …" He stopped, not knowing how to say it.

"Almost dead, … yes," she shared.

"And you can bring them back?"

"Not if they've already crossed over and gone. I'm not sure anybody can do that," she stated thoughtfully. "But I've definitely brought back some people who were pretty darn close to that line. They must really want to return to this plane though."

"Right," he noted. "I guess that makes the difference, doesn't it?"

"Yep, it sure does. If you've already crossed over and see everybody on the other side, everybody who you want to be with, it's very hard to convince you to come back here."

"Got it," he murmured. "I hadn't considered that."

"That's because you deal with sending people there." A

certain caustic tone was in her voice.

He blinked. "I gather that really bothers you."

"Nope." She shook her head. "I try hard not to get into that place about what bothers me, but I do have a certain awareness of what happens when you shoot and kill people. Believe me. Sometimes I understand they need to go where they're being sent, and other times it's just plain hard to sort out."

"Got it." Of course he didn't really. Not like he thought he should have, but she was certainly making him think, and that was worth a lot in itself. "I appreciate what you did for me," he said in a more formal tone.

That sent her off laughing again.

He frowned. "You're very unusual."

"I am, but I'm also just me." She shrugged. "When you get used to it, you'll be fine."

"Does it take a long time?" he asked, with that crooked smile.

"Maybe. Sorry. I'm not trying to be difficult, but I tend to be me all the time."

"Absolutely nothing is wrong with being you," he noted, "and I have to admit that I'm fascinated."

She gave him a look he didn't quite know how to interpret.

"You don't like that answer either. Why not?"

"It just reminds me of the fact that not everybody heals the same, and sometimes they wake up with this odd belief about who they are."

He just frowned at her. "What are you talking about?"

"I don't want any hero complex because I saved you," she murmured.

"Okay, got it." He smiled. "And I promise, I won't."

She searched his face for a long moment, "Good. Glad to hear that. Now you need to go back to bed."

"And if I don't want to?"

"Then don't," she replied. "It's up to you whether you want to heal and to join your friends again or to stay here even longer."

And what could he say to that? He groaned. "Okay, that's hard to argue with."

"It is, which is why I said it."

He carefully maneuvered his way back to the bed. "You said we would talk about options for getting me back on my feet."

"Tomorrow. Do as much healing as you can tonight, and we'll talk about it then."

And, with that, he had to be satisfied.

CHAPTER 2

CARA WOKE UP the next morning, wondering how Rick was faring. He was an interesting character, and, as she had told Terk, dangers were associated with what she did, but Terk had asked her specifically to try to help Rick, and she had agreed. She definitely found more problems than she had expected. They weren't necessarily insurmountable; they were just problems. She frowned as she got up, showered, then dressed and stepped out into the kitchen to find Rick sitting at the kitchen table in front of her laptop.

"I'm sorry for using your laptop without asking you first," he said, without looking up, "but I really needed to reconnect with the world and see what had gone to shit while I was out."

"Not a problem. Terk left it."

He nodded. "I figured as much. Fresh coffee's over there too."

"Good. Glad to see you can make a decent houseguest."

He burst out laughing at that. "I can be." He smiled, now focusing more on her. "I just didn't realize that would be a requirement."

"It's not," she replied, returning his smile, "but it certainly doesn't hurt." She stepped forward and poured herself a coffee. "Now, what do you want for food this morning?"

He shrugged. "Anything and everything. I'm just hungry, and it all sounds good."

With that, she cooked some bacon and eggs with toast. When she put a big platter down on the table between them, she watched his eyes light up. "You really are hungry."

He nodded. "Yep, I sure am."

He dug in, and she sat down with her much smaller portion. He wouldn't need her for very long after this, and, of course, that was where the problem came in. She figured it would be her problem, not his, and it was proving to be correct. As soon as he was done eating, he looked at her expectantly.

She nodded. "Let's get you through some physiotherapy moves." And again he absolutely amazed her with his resilience and ability to move and heal. She shook her head. "I've helped a lot of people, but nobody has had the level of recuperation abilities like you do."

"No, probably not. I'm *special*."

She burst out laughing. "Yes, you are." Cara was amused that he had chosen the exact replica of her own wording earlier. She smiled at him. "I'm really glad to see that you'll pick up your life, as you had hoped, physically. Now, what about the rest of it?"

"I haven't really tried," he admitted hesitantly.

"Well, everything else seems to be working, so there's a good chance that will be too."

"Maybe, I'm just not sure I want to test it yet."

She was surprised at that but nodded. "Whenever you're ready, Terk will probably test it more than you will."

"Yeah, I can see that he'll be on my case a little bit," he murmured.

"A little?" she asked in a droll tone.

Rick grinned. "Okay, so maybe a lot."

"He'll need to know what you can and cannot do, I would imagine."

"Yes and no," he replied, "and more than that. I think it'll be a case of whether I'm on the mend and can be of a help or not."

"You will be, one way or the other," she noted. "I just don't know to what extent."

He nodded. "Have you always been able to communicate like that?"

"You mean, telepathically? No, not always," she replied, but she didn't clarify. It wasn't a discussion she wanted to get into. Thankfully he accepted her response. She went through a series of exercises with Rick again, and he was getting stronger, almost by the minute. She checked her own energy, but he wasn't taking it from her, so that was good. She shook her head, when he was done. "You're pretty unbelievable."

"Nope. I'll put it down to good nursing."

She smirked. "Well, if I could take the credit, I would, but that's not my style."

He looked at her, grinned. "Hey, you're the one who kept me alive."

She *had* done that. "It took some of Terk's support too."

"Got it," Rick said. "That man and what he can do is absolutely amazing."

She nodded. "I hear you there."

As soon as lunch rolled around, he hopped to his feet, did a series of jumping jacks, and asked, "Food?"

She nodded. "Just sandwiches though. If you'll be leaving here soon, no sense in bringing in food. Every time we bring in a delivery, there's a chance of getting caught."

He frowned at that. "Have you had any trouble?"

"Not necessarily, but you never really know when your

luck is about to run out." He winced at that, and she knew he was thinking about the attack on the whole team.

"What have you had problems with?"

She told him about her last delivery, and one of the guys down the hallway, watching.

"Do you think he was an issue?"

"I don't know," she replied. "In all honesty, I'm not sure. He was definitely interested in what I was doing and the amount of food I was bringing in."

"And, of course, it's the amount that's always suspect, isn't it?"

"Well, I'm not a terribly large female, and I did bring in a lot of food on each delivery, mostly because I was trying not to have to go anywhere," she explained. "I do have groceries here to last quite a while longer, but, with you eating like you are, we'll need fresh fruit and veggies."

"And that'll mean another order."

"It also means you could be exposed to another potential attack, and I don't know whether the delivery guys even cared or if it was just curiosity."

"But you brought it up," he reminded her.

"Yes. My instincts say it wasn't casual."

"Did you tell Terk?"

"Yes." She nodded. "He said he'd take care of it."

Something was in her voice though. "You're worried about what Terk might have done to him?"

"Let's just say, I was worried that something might need to be done, and I really didn't want that on my conscience."

He agreed. "We normally don't kill people, unless it's in self-defense. Let's just park that for the moment. We'll eat what we have, and then, when we're ready to pull out, we'll make a good plan."

"We won't do that until we have a safe way to get you out of here."

He murmured, "Agreed. So we'll leave it at that, until Terk arranges for us to get out."

"Got it."

"And do you have any plans?"

"Nope, as I told you, Terk showed up out of the blue."

He laughed. "Yeah, that's our life. On the other hand, showing up out of the blue sounds like maybe it wasn't a problem."

"Nope, not at all," she stated. "I just had a change in my life, so I had an opening."

"An opening?"

"Yes. My last patient died."

He stared at her and slowly nodded. "Not exactly the highest recommendation."

"Surely not," she agreed cheerfully. "But, the fact of the matter is, not anything anybody could do. She'd been brain dead for a very long time."

"That's really sad," he murmured.

"Particularly for the family, who tried so hard to do everything they possibly could to keep her alive, but she just wasn't there to even assist anymore."

"And you knew she wasn't there?"

"Yes. She was long gone. I detected no soul activity left."

"Did you try to tell them that?"

"I did, but, of course, they didn't want to listen."

"Of course not. Anything else that you noticed around here?" he murmured.

"Do you mean, did anything else seem off?" She shrugged. "A couple things when I first got here. Almost as if the place were monitored, but I haven't seen any evidence of it."

"As long as nobody else is here, they'd think there's no change in my condition."

"If they even know you're here," she reminded Rick.

But he knew that they did. "No. They know."

She just stared. "Fine." She nervously looked at the door. "So, what are we expecting? Somebody to break through the front door or something?"

"I would hope not." Yet, as he stared at it, he realized it was all too likely. "Unfortunately I don't want to think about that, but it is possible."

She nodded. "And now that you mentioned it, I'm starting to feel that weird edge."

"When you say that, what do you mean?" he asked sharply.

She shrugged. "Just that sensation that …" She found she didn't know quite how to explain it.

"Has anybody else been in here besides me?"

"No. Only Terk. When we first got here, and he set me up. Beyond that, no."

"So, who set up the lease and everything like that?"

"Terk did."

He nodded. "And yet, like you, I'm starting to feel like something's going on out there."

"Well, definitely something's going on. It's just a matter of how much and how bad." She looked around. "I guess we need to be ready to leave fast too, don't we?"

"Yes."

"It would be better if you had a couple more days."

He tested out his own strength, nodded. "I know, but I'm not sure we'll get it."

Her gaze wide, she nodded. "In that case, I'll start packing."

He nodded and sat here with a cup of coffee and waited.

When she came back out a short while later, he asked, "All done?"

She nodded. "I didn't bring much."

"How long have we been here?"

"A couple weeks, and that's all I brought enough for anyway."

"Where's your bag?"

"It's sitting on my bed. Until we hear from Terk, I really don't have any authorization to change our status quo."

"Well, if it gets to the point of saving our lives, we won't have time to check in with Terk. We'll be doing whatever we need to, in order to keep ourselves safe."

She gave him a lopsided smile. "I didn't think we were in danger, until you woke up and started spouting all this stuff."

"Yes, you did," he disagreed quietly. "You've just been very good at holding off all the fear-mongering."

She giggled. "Yeah, not really my thing." She watched him carefully.

"So, what is it that you think you know when you look at me so intently?"

"You've come out of a coma after a traumatic event," she noted. "I always have to make sure that what comes out of your mouth is something that's believable."

He smiled. "Believe me. If our team had anybody else to assist you, then we would have them here," he murmured. "However, when danger happens, it doesn't exactly give us much warning."

"I know," she murmured. "Another reason why I'm here right now and listening."

And he realized that's literally what she was doing. "Good to know. When it happens, we need to run."

"And where will we run to?"

"Not sure yet." He smiled. "Let me contact Terk and see." He phoned Terk, and when he didn't get an answer right away, he frowned. "Now I don't like that."

"What's that?" she asked.

"No answer from Terk."

She frowned. "Are you seriously thinking something has happened?"

"When somebody wakes up like I have," he murmured, "all kinds of hell breaks loose because the people who are waiting for this to happen have just been alerted."

"Because you're awake, you mean?"

"Yes," he murmured. "Because I'm now awake, it's quite possible that we have awakened something else."

She stared at him in shock. "I don't think I like the sound of that. I came here to nurse somebody who needed my special brand of care."

"And you did," he agreed. "Now it'll be up to me to keep you alive long enough to get you out of here."

"What do you think they'll do if they find me?" she asked, staring at him.

"They'll make sure you can't tell anybody what you've been doing," he replied, "and that's only after they've extracted all the information they want."

She swallowed hard. "Damn. I was afraid you would say something like that."

"HEY," RICK REPLIED, "you saved my life. Trust that I'll do

everything I can to keep you safe."

"Oh, you will. I get that."

"That's not necessarily the answer I need to hear." He smiled. "You've been strong and brave so far. Let's not ruin it now."

She laughed. "No, of course not. Why would I show weakness? I mean, that sounds like a terrible idea." She gave him an eye roll.

He smiled at her. "Stand strong. We will get through this."

She nodded. "I have no doubt about it. It would just be nice if we could do it a little faster."

At that, he laughed. "As fast as I can."

"In that case, we need to get some more exercises done because you're still not quite up to snuff."

"It always hurts me when you say that," he noted. "I pride myself on being in perfect form."

"Well, too bad, because you're not there yet," she said caustically.

At that, he burst out laughing again.

"Let's go."

They went through several more rounds of therapy. By the time he was done, the exercise had sweat dripping off his forehead. "Good God. You're a taskmaster."

"I need to be because we need those muscles of yours up and running, as soon as they're able to."

"I thought we were doing just fine." He struggled with his breathing.

"You are. You're actually doing just fine," she confirmed, "but we have to do it for longer."

He groaned. "How about water first?"

She walked into the kitchen, came back with a bottle of

water, and handed it to him. As with everything he did, she watched him carefully.

"You really do have to ensure that everybody is fine, don't you?"

"Of course. Physiologically, you're still not there."

"Well, I hope you're wrong because we don't really have many options here."

"So far, we haven't had anything happen yet," she noted. "We're ready, and, if it needs to be today or tomorrow, obviously we'll do our best to make sure we stay ready."

"Yeah, but doing our best won't necessarily be enough."

She gave him a flat stare. "Until you tell us otherwise, there really is no other option."

Not a whole lot he could say to that. As soon as he got back on his feet, he had a shower and stepped into the kitchen. "I'll lie down, and then I'll try Terk again."

"If you do connect, make sure you grab some numbers of other team members, just so that, if we do get cut off, we aren't 100 percent cut off."

"Will do." Liking that she was thinking about the future ahead of them, Rick headed back to his room and laid down on his bed. Almost immediately he bolted to his feet and raced out to the living room. "Get ready to leave," he stated urgently.

She bolted to her feet and raced to the bedroom. "What's the matter?"

"Vehicles downstairs. Leave your bags. Don't argue." He barely managed to shove his feet into a pair of runners that were oddly enough just his size. He quickly led the way outside the apartment into the hallway. He looked down at his clothing. "Did you pick this out?"

"We needed something for you to sleep in," she explained. "I could have left you in pajamas, but I thought you would feel better in street clothing. Not to mention, it's perfect for the getaway."

Outside of her apartment, he led her in the opposite direction of the exit.

She pointed to it, but he shook his head. "We can't. They're coming that way." And, with that, he refused to even talk anymore and dragged her down and around to the next floor.

"Where are we going?" she asked, in a tightly controlled voice. But she wasn't out of breath, and she wasn't arguing with him.

"Not sure yet. You have any wheels here?"

"No, I don't," she murmured.

"Okay. I still haven't managed to get ahold of Terk."

"Neither have I," she stated flatly.

"It doesn't mean anything," he warned her, "and there could be any number of reasons."

She nodded. "None of them are good."

"That's not true."

Just then his phone rang. "That's Terk."

Terk said, "You need to move."

"We're on the stairwell, going down right now, and left our bags in the apartment, but we have no way to get out of here."

"Did you see them?"

"No," Rick replied. "I just felt them."

"Good. That's huge if your senses are on fire that much."

"Oh, they're on. Maybe too much. It's like little lightning jabs at my nerves."

"That's also good," Terk said. "We've talked about that

before."

"Sure, but that's when we had new abilities strengthening or coming into play. That's not what this is."

"Are you sure about that?" Terk asked, a cheery note to his voice. "Remember? I warned you that you could lose a few things, but you might also gain a few things."

"Well, I have no idea what I've got at the moment," he admitted, "except the need to survive. Cara is with me here. Can you send a ride for us?"

"Already on the way," he confirmed. "We'll be there in just a few minutes."

"I'll give you a location once we're out. I'm not even sure we can exit yet," he muttered. "I think they've got several vehicles outside. Presumably several men."

"I'll set up a diversion if there's time. We'll be on the opposite side of the street in a big black truck."

"Got it. What's your ETA?"

"We're still six minutes out," Terk replied.

"Make it four," Rick snapped. "We won't have much more time than that." As he hung up, he looked over at Cara. "Now you'll have to listen and do exactly what I say, when I say it."

She nodded. "I got it. I don't have a death wish."

"Glad to hear that. Come on." And, with that, he led her down to the main floor.

She asked, "Won't they find us here?"

"Absolutely they will. They'll start a search of the building here very soon. Once they check out the apartment and realize not only that we're gone but the teakettle is still hot, they'll be all over us."

She winced at that. "Not a good time to make a cup of tea, huh?"

"Doesn't matter. Our packed bags are evidence too. Almost always something's left behind for them to find. You can do your darndest, but it's almost impossible to completely escape without leaving any notice. And if you leave laptops behind…"

"Well, so far our exit has been fast enough," she murmured.

"We're waiting for Terk, that's all." Rick looked at her. "And you know Terk. He'll be here."

"Absolutely he will," she agreed, with spirit. "That's not my concern."

He stared at her and asked, "What is it then?"

"You," she replied. "You like to think that you're fully recovered, but I'm here to tell you that you're not."

"And how would you know?" he asked.

"I can see it in your energy."

He stopped midstep, then looked at her. "What do you see?"

"I see a man who's doing what he needs to do because he needs to do it, but he's also not recognizing the toll to his body."

"I don't have any choice." He grabbed her hand, turned, and raced down the stairs anyway.

"I know," she agreed. "That's why I didn't mention it before. No matter what I say, you'll still do you."

He looked at her, smiled. "You wouldn't have it any other way."

His words were something that she had to watch and to keep an eye on because he was right. She wouldn't have it any other way. However, so much was going on right now. He was still her patient, so, in her mind, her safety wasn't as important as his, but she didn't really want to check out right now either. She often told friends of hers that she was okay to check out whenever the time came because she knew what happened on the other side.

Yet she knew that her life wasn't over, and, even with family and friends waiting for her over the rainbow, she didn't want to check out early, not if she didn't have to. She would be damned if she would go like this. Not now. To have some asshole on their backs like this made her angry.

As they raced down the stairs and exited an unmarked side door, then headed out to the street, he tucked her close against him. "Pretend like we're a couple," he murmured.

She wrapped her arms around him. "Why?" she whispered.

"So they'll think we're together," he said. "They're looking for a nurse and her patient. So glad you don't wear scrubs, just for times like this."

She nodded. "Got it," she murmured. "I just want to get out of here safe."

"That's what I'm trying to do," he replied.

"I'm worried about you," she said, looking at him.

"Don't worry about me," he argued in a strong voice. "I'm fine."

"I am pleasantly surprised at that," she murmured, as they waited at the street corner.

His gaze was forever searching around here.

"I don't know how you can always search and not make it look like you're searching," she noted, "but, as I was saying, I'm quite pleased at how well you're healing."

"The healing was never in doubt," he murmured.

"*Not*," she snorted.

He stared at her for a moment. "That bad?"

She nodded. "You had one foot in the grave and don't

you ever forget it."

He gently hugged her. "And, for your healing gifts, I'm very grateful."

"I don't want your gratitude," she replied in a sharp tone. "It's a bit of a sore spot."

He nodded. "Got it. It won't be gratitude. I promise."

She smiled, just as the crosswalk light changed, and he ushered her firmly over to the other side.

"Any particular reason why we're here?"

"Because our ride will be here soon," he shared. "The least we can do is be on the correct side of the street when they arrive."

She looked around. "And yet I don't see anybody here to collect us."

"We don't want them to see us," he noted. "We just want it to be a smooth and easy transition. So you just keep looking around, like you're a tourist out for a nice little walk."

"Got it," she muttered.

And she could play the game as well as the next person. She just didn't like to do it. She wasn't about subterfuge and secrecy, being much more of a straight player.

"I get it," he told her. "This isn't your normal thing."

"No, it sure isn't," she murmured.

"But we had to get out of there."

"Are you sure they were even coming after you?"

"Nope, but I wasn't hanging around to find out either." He wasn't at all sure that these guys weren't coming after *her*, with her skill set.

"No, I can see that," she agreed. "At the same time, I was hoping that you would have a few more days."

"We didn't get it, and I'm not too anxious to go back in

there and try and get a couple more."

"No," she whispered. "I'm not either."

Behind them, they heard shouts. He pulled her closer and squeezed her. "Don't look." He moved her over to a bus stop bench, and they both sat.

"And how do you not look?" She struggling hard to not immediately turn to see what was going on.

"It could be anything. We have to make sure that it's nothing connected to us."

"Well, we won't do that if we don't look," she argued in exasperation.

He laughed. "I already know that it has to do with us. I can sense that much."

"So can I, but how can you just sit here and not look around to make sure they aren't coming up behind us?"

"That's what our Spidey senses are for, and mine is on strong alert right now."

"Maybe," she cautioned him, "but you've also been injured."

"Yep, I sure have been." He nodded. "Another reason why mine are on higher alert than normal. I would do a lot to avoid going back down again."

CHAPTER 3

CARA WATCHED, AS Rick searched the area calmly and effectively. "Nobody is here waiting for us," she noted. "Aren't they supposed to be here already?"

"They will be," he replied encouragingly.

"Says you," she muttered.

"This is my team. They won't leave me behind."

"No, I agree with that. Terk went to a lot of trouble to keep you alive."

"I know, but then Terk is also family."

"Like real family?"

"Better than real family." He smiled. "No, we aren't blood relations, though he does have a brother who is also in the industry."

"Right, that's interesting. Does he have the same kind of abilities?"

"I don't think so," Rick stated, "though I don't know that the discussion has ever come up."

"It must be hard to not be part of this, if everybody else around you has these crazy abilities."

"Maybe, or maybe he just doesn't care."

She didn't know what to think of that, and it wasn't even worth discussing right now. Yet she was happy for any conversation to take her mind off the fact that she knew they were being pursued and that, behind her somewhere, was somebody looking to put a bullet in her back.

"Do you think they want to kill us or do they want to take us?"

"Well, if I were them, I would want to take us," he shared, "but you can't ever really be sure."

"Right, and is this about confirming you're alive?"

"I think so," he replied, "and that may be of more value to them. Depends on what they did to try and kill us all," he added. "If the attack on us was just a test, then they know that they have to do something different to keep us down on a permanent basis."

"Or they're trying to figure out what kind of abilities you have that you could withstand what they already did," she suggested quietly.

"They didn't know I had a guardian angel," he murmured, squeezing her again.

She shook her head. "If they knew about Terk, they should know that *he's* the guardian angel, and he's the one who arranged all this."

"Yes, and they're probably assuming that already," Rick agreed. "We're trying to keep them from knowing anything for sure, and what they don't know won't hurt us."

"Got it," she murmured. "I'd still feel better if we weren't sitting out in the open."

"Where would you like to go?" he asked.

"I don't know. Maybe over in that corner over there." She pointed to a doorway alcove.

"Considering that the wind has come up, I'm good with that." They walked over and stood in the shelter there.

"How much longer do you think?" she murmured.

"Terk said they were six minutes out."

"It's been ten minutes."

"I know, but, if they're smart, they're doing some reconnaissance, ensuring they're not driving into a trap."

She shivered at that. "It's quite the life you live."

"It's the life we live, but it wasn't the life we were used to," he stated. "You never really know where the attacks come from now. We thought we were safe. We thought we were just being officially disbanded by our government. Black ops and all, but we were all prepared to go off and have a life after this. Whoever attacked my team are the ones who changed that," he added almost viciously.

She nodded. "So, is this about revenge for you guys?"

He shook his head. "Absolutely not, but it is about ensuring that we're safe and aren't doing everything based on having to deal with these guys. We have to take them off our backs, and, in order to do that," he stated, "we have to solve this and figure out who is behind it. Then we take appropriate measures so that they can't come after us anymore."

"I know it sounds good in theory and all that, but so many things can go wrong."

"Things can always go wrong," he confirmed, his voice calm and steady.

"How can you be so calm?" she cried out softly in frustration.

He looked at her, with a smile. "Because I've been here before. I've seen it happen, time and time again."

"And were you the one who was being hunted?" she asked.

"No, not necessarily," he replied, "but it's amazing what you can get used to."

"This isn't the kind of life I would like to get used to," she stated immediately.

"I got it," he agreed, "which is also why I'm doing the

best I can to see that you survive this and can go on and do whatever it is that's at the top of your wish list."

She nodded.

Just then a vehicle came up in front of them.

He looked at it. "Bingo. Here we go."

She held on to his arm, as he pulled her forward. "Are you sure?" she asked.

"Yes. Aren't you?"

She looked at it, then nodded. "Okay, it has the right energy."

He nodded and quickly led her to the vehicle. The door opened automatically, and, just as they went to step inside, shouts came all around them. She was basically picked up and tossed inside, and Rick followed, as the vehicle took off at an alarming pace.

When it slowed down ever-so-slightly, one of the men in the front seat turned, looked at her with a smile, and introduced himself. "Hi. I'm Wade." He pointed to his passenger. "This is Damon."

She nodded faintly. "I'm Cara," she whispered. "Where are we going?"

"Someplace safe," Wade replied gently. "Don't you worry. Terk will do what it takes to keep you alive."

At that, Rick reached over, laced his fingers with hers. "So will I. We'll be fine. Just hold tight, Cara, while we get through this."

She nodded. "I put my trust in you guys a while ago. It hasn't been wrong yet."

RICK WATCHED CARA'S interaction with the others in the

vehicle. She seemed a little overwhelmed, but he held on to her, and he had to respect that nothing was easy about what had just happened. He squeezed her hand. "It'll be fine. I promise."

She gave him a ghost of a smile. "You're not in any position to promise anything," she murmured.

He grinned. "Hey, maybe not, but I've already beaten the odds." At that, she shot him a look that he wasn't exactly sure how to interpret, so he stayed quiet. After several minutes and several elaborate driving maneuvers, they took a few corners at a more normal speed.

"Did you lose the tail?" Rick asked Wade.

"We think so," he responded, "but it's a little hard to tell at the moment. We'll keep driving around a bit to double-check."

Rick didn't say anything, knowing how the system worked. Cara, on the other hand, didn't seem to have the same confidence. She looked a little more worried the longer they were out. "It's okay," he whispered to her. "They're just being cautious."

"Are you certain?" she murmured. "It seems like we're not getting anywhere very quickly."

"Except for the tail," he noted. "Once they get rid of that, we'll be free and clear."

"I hear that. I'm just not so sure I believe it."

He smiled. "You know what? Being a doubting Thomas has probably held you in good stead all this time"—he paused—"but there are times when it's better to trust."

She didn't respond.

He wondered about the reticence that he felt in her, that sense of holding something back. Something deep inside. But she was already somebody he wasn't used to because how many people out there had the skills that she had? Yet they shared an instinctive bond, after what they'd been through.

Yet, if she had been contacted by Terk a long time ago, why had she chosen not to go into this line of work? Almost immediately the answers slammed into his brain. Espionage was definitely not for the faint of heart, and neither was it for those who wanted to live a life of healing. Which, as a nurse, obviously that had been her first choice.

She had to be wondering how she had ended up in this nightmare, though he remembered something she'd said about owing Terk a favor. And Terk was like that. He knew people all over the world. People who cared, people who seemed indebted to him for work he had done in some shape or form. And that made sense too. Terk's team saw grateful people all over the world, and it was quite amazing to see just what the results of Terk's team's work could entail sometimes.

Rick settled back, as the vehicle made a series of sudden sharp turns, and then, all of a sudden, they looked to be inside a massive garage. He looked around in surprise. "Have you guys set up a new compound?"

"Somewhat," Wade replied. "It would be a lot easier if we were setting up on a permanent basis, but it seems like we're just trying to stay ahead of the attacks."

At that, he felt Cara at his side, her fingers trembling.

He squeezed the hand he still hadn't let go of and murmured, "It's all right." She didn't say anything but clung to his hand, and, for that, he was thankful. That contact alone should help her to feel a little better at least. He understood that he really had come into this work lightly. Hell, in his case, he'd come into it without any real options.

He'd been so busy trying to stay alive with his own abilities and doing the work that he thought needed to be done that Terk had been a godsend. Their team had set into this work willingly, but Rick also knew that it wasn't for everyone.

"This is really a temporary residence and our headquarters," Wade explained.

Rick looked around at the huge set of warehouses and nodded. "It might be temporary, but it's not a bad solution at all. I'd imagine it's got more than a few people confused."

"Well, we hope so. It just seems like we never quite get anywhere with these guys."

"Well, I'm here to help now, as much as I can," Rick stated, "so maybe we can get back to using some of our senses."

"That would be nice," Damon noted, joining the conversation. "We've missed your grounding abilities."

"Yeah," Wade agreed. "Not being able to power up is hugely frustrating."

"I know," Rick added. "I've been dealing with that myself."

As they all exited the vehicle, Rick kept Cara close. "I know that you don't want to be here," he murmured to her. "But we need to keep you here, until we know what's up."

She just shot him a look and then shrugged. "I trust Terk, but I'm not so sure about everybody else."

He frowned at that. "Well, it's Terk's team," he murmured. "So, in theory, if you trust Terk, you should trust his team, since he personally handpicked all of us."

"I get that," she whispered in a low voice. "It's just strange to see so many people all at once."

"I think you're just used to that single-patient lifestyle."

She smiled at that. "Generally I work with only one patient, and then something happens, and they either come back to life or not, and so I move on."

He nodded slowly. "I get that. Believe me. I appreciate all you've done for me, and I don't want to see anything happen to you now, especially from an association with me."

"Neither do I," she stated with spirit, "so it's up to you guys to keep me safe."

"Got it." He chuckled. "I really don't think that will be a problem."

She shrugged. "At least you're confident," she murmured. "I'm not so sure that it's justified yet, but, hey, let's see what everybody has to say and what's been going on."

Together, they followed the men into a series of rooms. "This is a huge space," she noted. "You could have people hidden all over in here, and nobody would ever know."

"Very true," he commented.

"And it would be unusual to have that much open space and not in use. And yet that's what this appears to be." She turned, looking at him.

"And I'll find out why and how," he stated. "Don't you worry."

Almost immediately upon entering the main computer room, he was engulfed in hugs. He quickly wrapped Tasha in his arms and gave her a gentle hug. "Hey, am I ever glad to see you. I didn't even ask Terk if everybody made it," he admitted. "I assumed everybody did, but I hadn't really realized until I saw you just now."

She nodded. "Some didn't make it. Mera and Wilson both were killed."

He stared at her in shock, as she nodded.

"I don't know how much Terk has told you, but, after the attack on the team, they came gunning for the three of us admins in our homes, and they were the first two casualties. It's a miracle they didn't get me."

By the time he caught up on the rest of the news, he was incredibly angry and overwhelmed. The only thing that kept him from losing it entirely was knowing that Cara was at his side, hearing it all as well. And, for her, this was even more shocking.

She finally spoke up. "Please tell me that you'll catch these guys."

"That's the plan." Terk walked in behind her. He smiled at her gently.

She walked over and gave him a big hug, with deep affection. When she stepped back, she looked up at him. "What trouble did you get me into?"

"Trouble we'd hoped we could keep you out of," he admitted, "but we always knew it was a possibility, once Rick woke up."

She sighed. "Hard to believe that keeping him in a coma would have been a better idea."

"He was ready to come out. He was starting to fight it."

"If you say so," she said. "I know he was still holding and probably could have stayed for a while longer."

Rick stared at her in shock. "I might have been able to, but I sure as hell didn't want to."

"Which is also why I told Terk that it was time."

At that, the others crowded around. "I don't understand," Sophia admitted. "Rick, were you able to come out of the coma on your own?"

"No," Cara interrupted immediately, before Rick had a chance to reply. "He hadn't healed sufficiently, so we were keeping him in an induced coma until he was stronger." He stared at her in shock. She shrugged. "It's fairly typical in medicine," she murmured.

He nodded. "I know. I just didn't realize that's what you were doing." Then he stopped, looked down at his arms, seeing strap marks, where he had been held in place. His gaze shot over to her. She gave him a bland smile. He narrowed his gaze. "We'll have to talk later."

"Yep," she replied easily, "one day."

Which, to Rick, also meant that she had no intention of entering such a discussion until she was ready. Rick looked back over at Terk to see the corner of his lips twitching. "So I gather this was something you guys cooked up on your own?" he asked in amazement.

"Not quite," Terk stated, "but, while you were in your coma, you were sending out all kinds of signals that were quite likely to get you unwelcome attention. And we couldn't have anything happen to you or have anybody know where you were located," Terk explained. "So I had to keep some of your energy shattered in order to have you heal, without sending out all those crazy signals."

Rick shook his head. "I didn't even know I was doing that," he murmured.

"Exactly. That's what I'm saying. Since you didn't know what you were doing, and we were still all under attack, I had to do everything I could to keep you all safe," he stated. "So a coma was the best answer, and, even then, we were shutting down as much of your communication ability as possible."

"And that's what she did, wasn't it?" he asked, releasing her hand, not saying her name, not quite sure how to keep his tone from being harsh, but, in a way, it felt like a betrayal.

Terk immediately raised an eyebrow. "Cara did that to a

certain extent for your own benefit." Rick frowned at that. Terk immediately shook his head. "Definitely for your own benefit," he repeated, with a word of warning in his voice. "Don't even begin to think otherwise."

"It just doesn't feel quite right."

"If you had only seen the shape you were in," she added quietly, "you wouldn't have argued."

He sighed and nodded. "Of course that's something I didn't know, but it feels more like I was being kept against my will."

She snorted at that. "I disagree, unless keeping you alive and keeping you safe is punishment to you."

"I get it. I get it," Rick said, now facing her. "Sorry. I didn't mean to imply that you'd done something wrong."

"Good," she snapped, her tone short, "because that is something I won't tolerate."

At that, the others looked at her with surprise.

He sighed. "You all have no idea what she's like," he teased, with an eye roll.

"And, if they're lucky, they won't need to engage with me as their nurse," she declared in an equally crisp tone, "because they won't be in the same condition you were in."

"And I get it," he stated. "I apologize if I made it sound like you were holding me against my will."

"Yeah, that's *exactly* what you said, and I'm telling you right now that I'm not putting up with that. Terk, could you please find a way to get me home again."

"Where is home anyway?" Wade stepped in curiously.

She looked at him. "Liverpool since a few years."

He frowned. "That shouldn't be too hard." Then he looked back over at Terk. "Or is it?"

"We should all be home again," Terk commented.

"What I don't know is whether our friend Rick here is capable of being on his own right now," Terk stated, his gaze direct.

She frowned, then looked over at Rick and shrugged. "He thinks he is."

"Just because he thinks he is," Terk noted, with a note of amusement, "doesn't mean anything, as you and I both well know."

She groaned. "Then the honest answer is no, he's not. But he won't let me do anything, and we've brought him out of his coma, so he can do whatever the hell he wants to now." It was obvious she was still really pissed.

Shaking his head, Rick looked over at Terk. "I don't get it."

"Of course not," Terk stated, "because you have no idea just how much Cara's been involved in keeping you alive."

"Or that you've been keeping him safe," she added. Terk nodded slowly.

"Of course," Rick admitted, "but sounds like none of the team really knew the full extent of that."

She looked at Rick, then around at the others. "You do all realize that Terk's been keeping all your energy up and heavily focused on healing, while at the same time keeping shields up, trying to guard you all, right?" she snapped, her hands on her hips, as she glared at each and every one of them. "So, if any one of you thinks that you're doing this all on your own, you're wrong. It's been Terk the whole way."

CHAPTER 4

CONSIDERING THE SPEED with which Cara had been ushered out of the main room into a room of her own, she figured that the team had decided to take matters into their own hands and to have private discussions without her. She couldn't blame them, but, at the same time, it felt odd.

She'd been part of Rick's life for the last couple weeks, at a very deep level. She knew the danger of becoming too attached. But she couldn't do this work by staying detached. When she left herself open at that level, all kinds of things could happen. She should have expected this, and, in a way, she did. It was a hard reality, and she would just have to accept the facts of life in her world right now.

In this case, a little more so than usual, and that was her own fault. She shouldn't have gotten this heavily involved in his care, but it had been necessary in order to keep him alive. She walked over to the bed in her new room and sat down, wondering what she was supposed to do now. She was tired, but it was more than the effects of the adrenaline that had kicked in and dissipated. She was tired inside and out. She'd been on full watch for a very long time, and, as always, when this kind of change happened in her system, she felt the need for a break on all levels.

She had an en suite bathroom, so she walked in and washed her face, as she contemplated what she was supposed to do next, now that she had time on her hands. Could she just walk out of here and expect them to let her go? Would Terk keep everything floating energy-wise without her? She hoped so because she didn't necessarily want to stay here. Being a useless wheel at this point in time in her life wasn't a goal. She wanted to move on and to find something useful to do again.

She had known that Rick wouldn't be with her forever, but she hadn't expected her care to come to such an abrupt end either. Yet she knew Terk well enough to know that absolutely nothing was ever normal around him, at least not in the few dealings she'd had with him.

He'd been a huge help to her at one point in time, and she'd been more than happy to help him out this time, but what was she to do now? Stumped, she curled up on the bed, wondering if she could possibly sleep, but her nerves were jangled. Everything was too stirred up to relax enough to actually let go. Trust was a hard thing, and, when you were like her, it was even harder.

When a knock came on her door, she said, "Come in." She sat up to see Rick entering, a cup of coffee in his hand. "Is that for me or for you?" she asked in a wry tone.

He smiled. "For you of course."

She nodded. "Ah, so the tables have turned, have they?"

"Maybe." He shrugged. "Would that be so wrong?"

"I don't know," she said. "I don't really know what that feels like."

He stopped for a moment on his way toward her and then took several more steps. "Maybe it's time you found out."

"Maybe." She sighed. "It's never been an issue either way."

He frowned. "It doesn't seem like something that would be a problem for you." She looked at him, silently questioning him. "Obviously I don't know you all that well in some ways, but I do feel like I know you in others."

She laughed. "A lot of that is the energy work. It's very deceptive."

"Maybe not," he argued. "One of the things that we learn with Terk all the time is that he doesn't lie, so when you do find things on an energy level, you're getting more of a truth than you were expecting."

She nodded. "And that's a good lesson to learn," she agreed, with a serious tone. "It's not that easy to learn either, so if you can do it now, all the better."

"And you have obviously had a lot more energy experience than I had any inkling of."

She shrugged. "Doesn't matter though, does it? Have you found a way to get me home again?"

"No, and honestly we have some concern that you may not be safe. Once these bad guys track down who was with me in that apartment, it won't be hard for them to find you." He hesitated and then sat quietly beside her. "Did you leave anybody in Liverpool who might become a target?"

She stared at him for a long moment, then slowly shook her head. "Meaning, do I live alone? Yes, I do. Do I have friends and family there? No, not really," she murmured. "Almost all my friends and family are gone."

"I'm sorry," he said. "I didn't want to ask that question, but I needed to."

"And I appreciate you thinking about other people in my life, but I came over here to do a job, and I wasn't expecting to stay over here beyond the end of it."

"We'll get you back safe and sound as soon as we can. I

promise.”

She stared at him. “But you can’t really promise that, can you? Not honestly. That attack at the apartment was no fluke, and they were looking for you.”

“I think they were looking for any activity that would confirm that I was still alive. And, as each of us comes out of the coma,” he shared, “they’re hunting for the others even harder.”

She considered him for a moment, seeing and hearing some truth to his words. “It also explains why Terk is trying to bring people closer together geographically, so he can keep his energy focused on one area and not split apart,” she murmured.

“Yeah, that makes perfect sense,” Rick agreed. “Look. I don’t even know how much of this latest hunt by the bad guys had you as a target, but we don’t want anything to happen to you. Especially not after you were such a huge help to me.”

“Ah, so you’re really keeping me alive out of gratitude, *huh*?” she asked, with a cheeky grin.

He seemed startled by her comment; then he shook his head and froze. “I don’t even know how to take that. I mean, obviously I’m delighted that you’re not overwrought and crying like many women would be in this situation, but I certainly don’t want you to think that we’re taking any of this lightly.”

“No, I know that,” she said. “But, while I’m here, is there anything I can do? I need to be busy, and I’ll go stir crazy if I’m not.”

“A couple of us are putting together a meal right now.”

“Why you? Why are you not resting?” she asked, giving him a hard look.

"Because, like you, I felt like I needed to do something. Everybody else has already been living a life for the last few weeks, while I was under whatever coma you guys deemed safe for me," he noted, with an eye roll. "I feel like I'm late to the mission, and now it feels like I have a lot to make up for."

"I get it," she stated, "but that doesn't mean you need to do it all at once."

He looked at her. "I know. Really I do, but, at the same time, it seems odd to be back in the land of the living and not doing anything. I was always a doer. I was always busy. I was involved pretty heavily. So to find the guys here are ahead of me in *this*, whatever the hell happened," he explained, "it feels like I need to play catch up."

She nodded. "So you go from being a coma patient to cooking dinner in what, two days?"

He smiled. "I did warn you that I heal fast."

"There's healing fast, and then there's healing fast."

"We'll chalk it up to your skills then," he teased, with a bright smile.

"You mean, to the energy work?"

"You and I will have to talk about that"—he gave her a hard look—"because I had no idea that you were doing anything."

"So what difference does it make?" she asked.

With that, he shrugged, then attempted to turn and leave.

She hopped up, coffee in hand. "Let me help with dinner at least."

"You could try just relaxing for once," he suggested. "You worked hard looking after me."

She smiled. "I don't know how much hard work that

was," she murmured, "but I like to be busy." He frowned, but she walked past him and out of the room. "If you guys are done with your private discussion," Cara said, "then no reason why I can't come out and join you, is there?"

Rick asked, "What private discussion?" But a note of humor was in his voice.

She looked at him and smiled. "Exactly."

He laughed and walked her into the main computer room. "She doesn't want to stay in her room," he announced. "She wants to help."

At that, one of the other women—Tasha, she thought—looked up and smiled. "Welcome back," she said.

Cara smiled. "I figured if I gave you guys enough private time to have your secret talks, then maybe I would be welcome afterward."

After that came a moment of silence, then Terk started laughing. "As if it'll do any good with you."

She smiled. "But at least it gives you the *semblance* of privacy."

At that, Damon frowned. "I'm sorry, but we need to be filled in on exactly what's going on here."

Terk shrugged. "I asked her to look after Rick because of his particular state. She has energetic and healing abilities that he needed most desperately."

"When you say that"—Rick stared, his gaze going from Cara to Terk—"was I in worse shape than the others?"

"No, not necessarily worse, but you were rattled in a different way. Each of you needed very different things. In your case, it was all about energy, and that's what we were trying to preserve."

"My senses?" he asked.

Terk nodded. "Yes, exactly. I'm not sure if that would

have mattered to you that you still had your senses when you woke up, but I was pretty sure that it would impact your life forever to lose them permanently."

"I never thought about it like that," Rick admitted. "I just assumed we were all in the same boat." He turned to look at Cara, as she sat nearby, studying the curious faces around her. "You told me that you owed Terk a favor."

"He'd been a big help at one point in time in my life," she stated. "So, when he called, I didn't have any reason to turn him down, and it gave me the opportunity to pay him back."

"And you do know that no payback was required," Terk murmured.

She shrugged. "Not everybody sees a debt as a requirement to be paid," she noted, "but, when somebody calls for help, it's part of my nature to respond."

"And that"—Terk nodded—"is quite accurate. She is a nurse and has a history of working with people in long-term comas."

At that, Rick faced Cara. "You did mention something about that. When you looked after a patient, it could go either way."

"Sure," she agreed. "It all entirely depends on how much of their cord is still functioning and how much they actually are still invested."

"And you can tell that?" Sophia asked, astonished.

She nodded. "In Rick's case, his cord was already partially severed."

Silence swept the room.

ALTHOUGH RICK HAD heard her mention that before, he hadn't really recognized the relevance of it, but, as soon as he heard the words yet again, he understood. "And so, you did what you could to save me." He nodded. "Thanks for that."

"Not sure that thanks are needed," she noted. "I did what I could do. I didn't know anything about the situation you were in until Terk here contacted me, and then I came, and luckily you're still with us."

"And mostly intact," he added, with an eye roll.

She grinned. "Well, there's nothing we can do about the core personality."

He stared at her for a moment, and then his laughter burst free. "Oh my, definitely a breath of fresh air." He looked at the others, who were still staring at both of them curiously.

"I didn't even know something like that was possible," Lorelei noted quietly.

"You never really know what's possible until you find an area that you specialize in and see what you can do to help. I've brought back quite a few coma victims," Cara murmured, "but I can't help all of them."

"No, of course not. Nobody can. The fact that you could even help Rick is wonderful, and thank you for that," Tasha said immediately. "Now, Cara, if we can get you back home, safe and sound, I'll feel like we haven't taken advantage of you."

Cara laughed. "That's what people do. You take advantage and hope that it doesn't appear that way."

They looked at her in surprise.

Cara shrugged. "I mean, I came because Terk needed me, but did he take advantage of me? Potentially. Did I care? Not really, because I knew what I was doing was important."

"And we appreciate that," Terk stated.

She smiled. "And I know you do. I could also tell from Rick's energy that he was a strong person and that he was quite likely to survive. It's very depressing to work with patients and to know that they're already mostly gone and don't have the energy or the will to come back."

At that point in time, Terk stepped up. "Well, all that is very interesting, but what it doesn't do is help us get out of this mess."

"And is getting out of this mess what we're after?" Cara asked, looking at him. "I assumed you already had a dozen plans in that head of yours."

He nodded. "I do, at least a dozen plans, but that doesn't mean any of them will come to fruition."

"Nope, but I trust that you will do what you need to do or what you see as the best course of action," she murmured.

"I'd like to hope so," he noted, "but, as you and I both know, that doesn't always come to pass."

"All right, there's an awful lot of innuendo happening here," Sophia stated. "No offense intended, but would somebody mind filling us in, so that we're not guessing?"

Terk shrugged. "I helped her brother at one point in time, and, through that, I found her abilities. I tried to recruit her to the team, but she wasn't having anything to do with it."

At that, the team turned to look at her.

Rick smiled, as he reached over, patted her hand. "Our loss, but I'm very grateful that, when Terk called on you again, you accepted the challenge."

She nodded. "At the same time, I had to make some decisions as to what I wanted to do about my future."

"I don't understand that part." Sophia sat at her computer, her arms crossed, still staring at her. "How does that affect your future?"

"Well, because it was obvious that Rick was in danger, so I knew it was quite possible that he would be hunted while he was comatose. Therefore, it would take some time and effort to keep him safe."

At that, Damon whistled. "Oh, my God. You're a guardian, aren't you?"

"Well, that's not a term I've used very much," she admitted, "but, technically speaking, yes."

The others erupted in a clamor of exclamations.

"What does that even mean?" Lorelei cried out. "Somebody needs to explain it to me because I don't understand very much of this at all." She looked over at Cara and added, "Sorry. I'm the least acquainted with all this energy stuff. I work for the government and, of course, knew the team and all, but I didn't know all the details and the particulars. Enough to get me targeted but not enough to understand."

"Interesting." Cara studied her face. "Because you have quite a bit of talent yourself."

Lorelei stared at her in shock. "What are you talking about?"

"You," she began. "You have the ability to communicate on another level, don't you?"

She flushed. "Yes, but only with him." She said, pointing to Gage.

"Well, that's just because that's where your focus is," Cara stated calmly. "You could open that up to the rest of the team, I'm sure. The men are linked, and that makes it much easier to link to them."

"Oh." Lorelei sat back and stared at her. "So, you can do a lot of what they do?"

"I can do a lot of things," Cara admitted calmly, "but it's not something that I actually cultivate, only in terms of the patients I work with."

"Could you explain that?"

She shrugged. "I can, if we need to."

Just then came a terrible noise, an alarm, coming from one of the computers. Instantly the focus shifted from getting to know Cara to complete attention on the alarm system. Tasha had joined Sophia at the computers, and they were intently working at something. Rick watched in understanding, then leaned over when he saw the confusion and panic on Cara's face. "It's an alarm system they have set up."

"I get that," she murmured, "but is it a good thing or a bad thing?"

He laughed. "I'm saying both because nobody is in a panic yet."

At the word *yet*, she winced.

He nodded. "We do have a lot of systems in place, so we'll get to a full explanation as time moves on."

"We don't have to do all the explanations right now," she agreed calmly, "but, if nobody is running and bolting, what are we doing for food?"

They'd forgotten all about it in the midst of their discussion. "There was talk of starting a stir fry, but I'm not sure."

Just then, Mariana walked into the room, carrying a little boy. Cara stopped and stared. The little boy looked at her, and a smile crossed his face, and he wiggled from his mother's grasp and opened his arms. Wordless, Cara walked over, picked him up, and he threw his arms around her and held her close.

Rick whispered, "What the hell?"

At that, Cara looked back at him. "Children. Their energy is pure. He has no judgment. He comes from heart." She murmured, "They are the best things possible for healing." She looked over at the woman who joined them.

Mariana nodded, a bemused look on her face. "I am surprised. Little Calum has never reacted like that to anybody that I know of. He is typically a little more reticent with new people. I'm Mariana, by the way."

"And he might be again," she agreed gently. "It's literally just a case of him recognizing energy—good healthy healing energy—and knowing that I'm not an enemy. I'm Cara," she added, with a smile, as she cuddled the boy.

"It's a hard thing to think that my son doesn't already judge people because he has seen enemies everywhere," she noted, frowning.

"Oh, I don't know if that's the case, as much as just the fact, in that moment, he recognized a kindred soul," Cara explained.

At that, the woman nodded in relief. "I hope that's the explanation. I've never seen him respond like that. The alarm woke us up, but thankfully that's been shut down." She looked over at the others. "Is it anything to worry about?"

"I had set up a series of tripwires on people searching for us online," Sophia replied, sitting at the computer. "Somebody tripped them."

"Well, good. You tend to that, while I'll head into the big kitchen and get some food going," Mariana stated. "But I'll see if I need anything from our makeshift kitchen first."

"Perfect." Sophia snorted. "I suspect you're a hell of a lot better at cooking than I am."

At that, everybody seemed to find a job to do. Cara walked over with the little boy in her arms, and Rick watched in amazement as the two of them carried on a conversation that nobody else seemed to even follow. He looked at Terk. "Did you know about this?" he asked, motioning at the two of them.

"No, but I'm not surprised," Terk noted. "Children are like that."

"Everybody keeps saying children are like that. But like what? What does that mean?" Rick asked. "I guess I don't have any experience with children to understand."

Mariana laughed. "Well, this is Little Calum," she said, as she introduced them. "And, yes, Cal is his father. My son is four years old and quite a handful. He also seems extremely intelligent."

"Well, if he's Calum's, of course he is." Rick immediately defended his friend. "I don't think I've ever actually met this little guy."

"No, it's the first that we've been together around your team," she shared. "Somebody was trying to get at Calum and kidnapped the two of us. That's one of the things you missed out on while you were unconscious."

"Right." He frowned, hating to hear what she'd been through. "I'm sorry that happened. It doesn't sound like an easy time for you."

"It wasn't easy for any of us," she agreed, "but much harder for this little guy." She nodded toward where Little Calum was curled up, listening to Cara talk to him about food. "She's pretty special if she has that kind of effect on kids," Mariana murmured to Rick.

He nodded. "She's had a pretty special effect on me too. I just wasn't sure whether it was energy or reality."

Mariana laughed. "Honestly I think they're the same thing at this point in time."

He stared at her in confusion.

She shrugged. "I only ever learned to communicate because of my link to Cal," she explained. "When he went down, Terk told me that he was dying and that he needed every bit of thought, positive thinking, prayer, whatever I could offer, to help keep him on this planet. Well, I wasn't about to let go in any way, shape, or form, so I fought for him, and maybe it wasn't a methodology that anybody else would agree with or something I even knew how to do," she added. "Yet something was pushing me, and suddenly I knew what to do and how to do it. I basically just stopped in my tracks, dropped, closed my eyes, and started to contact him, telling them how important he was to us and that we needed him."

Rick hadn't realized that everyone was listening in, but it seemed like little was private here.

Cara nodded. "And often that's all it is. You find out over time that people are listening, on a spirit level, and that they don't want to be lost to whatever nightmare they're caught up in. So, good for you for helping him to come back out of it again."

Mariana smiled. "And we're back together. And hopefully Cal has come to his senses about staying apart to keep us safe, and now we can move forward from this as a family. It is strange to think that, if all this hadn't happened, we would still be apart."

"Well, clearly it was intended to happen." Cara gave Mariana a big smile.

"Are we really thinking the government attacked our team, at least initially?" Rick asked, still struggling to get his mind wrapped around everything.

"It's definitely a consideration," Terk replied.

Rick looked around him at the ever-growing group. "And you guys have been here ever since you woke up?" A part of him was insanely jealous. He'd missed out on so much. Not just the work they'd done but watching the family grow.

"Yes," Terk replied, "though we started in only a tiny part of this building. But, as we expanded into having more and more people here, we needed more space, better facilities, and better capability in terms of keeping the food and all that is required to keep everybody safe."

"And how are we handling deliveries, if nobody is to know that we're here?" Rick asked.

"Well, that's the trick," Wade replied. "On paper, this whole property is rented to a few different companies. We do have to go out every once in a while, and, when we do, it takes quite a bit of planning and preparation to keep everybody safe."

Rick nodded. "Well, it would be good for me to test my abilities in that area. So the next time somebody needs to do something, let me know, so I can try out the grounding."

"Will do," Terk noted.

At that, Damon walked over. "He says that, but he doesn't mean it."

Rick looked at him and asked, "What do you mean?"

"He won't put you to a test until he thinks that you're much stronger." Damon looked over at Terk in time to see his lips twitch. "You know, Terk? You're the product of your own problem. You don't want to let us go," Damon murmured.

"No, I sure don't," Terk agreed. "You're all way too valuable to me to lose you over something so simple."

"It's not simple if I can help keep these guys alive," Rick

argued. "Why won't you let me try?"

"Because you're not strong enough."

And there, once again, was a blunt assessment of Rick's abilities, without even giving him a chance to prove otherwise. He felt his temper rising. "You don't know that," he replied stiffly.

Terk looked at him flatly for a long moment. "Yes, I do. And, as soon as you're ready, believe me. We'll put you to work. But, in the meantime, no."

And, of course, Terk wasn't used to being argued with or ignored, and, when he put his foot down, almost nobody ever went against him. It was pretty hard to since he always had logic and reason on his side. Still, right now, it was all about something completely different.

"I don't get it," Rick admitted. "What are you afraid of?"

"That something will take you out that you're not quite ready for."

"And what is that?" he asked. "If there's something going on here that I don't understand, you guys need to fill me in. Otherwise I'm just out here in the dark."

Terk shook his head. "We've brought you up to speed. Now rest." This time, he wouldn't hear any arguments.

Rick collapsed in a chair and glared, and then caught sight of the grin on Cara's face. He upped the wattage of his scowl.

She shrugged. "Doesn't work on me. I'm immune."

"Immune to what?" he asked in astonishment.

"To your antics. I've seen them all."

And with that stunning announcement, she handed off Little Calum. "I'll be back in a few minutes."

CHAPTER 5

C ARA WAS PROBABLY saying more than she should, but it was hard when she saw the interactions going on around her. These men had been through so much and still had so much to offer; yet it was fascinating to see the team dynamics and to see how Terk still ruled everything, as if he had no need to explain to anyone the whys of what he was doing. And maybe he didn't.

Maybe the team was good with that, but she wasn't so sure. The more she saw the reactions of some of the men, silently questioning Terk's lack of explanation, she could understand that. Everybody wanted to know why they were doing something, even if they didn't actually have a particular reason. She went to use the washroom and wandered around the large warehouse complex, looking out the window every once in a while. As she slowly returned, some of her restlessness eased inside.

Terk looked at her and asked, "Better?"

She nodded. "Yes, thanks."

He nodded. Nobody else really seemed to know what to say.

Cara felt their silent questions overwhelming her. "Terk and I have known each other for a long time," she stated quietly. "He just knew I was feeling restless."

"No wonder," Tasha agreed. "Sorry about all the problems.”

“Me too,” she murmured. “I’d like to be on my way home and not have to worry about any of this, but obviously that won’t be a part of the plan. At least not today.”

“No, I don’t think so,” Terk confirmed.

And the women all turned from their computers and smiled. “But that doesn’t mean staying here will be all that terrible.”

“I hope not.” Cara walked over to the kitchen table and sat down. Almost immediately Little Calum was there beside her. She smiled at him. “What would you like?” And he just reached up his arms. She picked him up and held him close. She looked over at Mariana. “You’re truly blessed to have him.”

Mariana nodded. “I am, although he’s definitely been surprising me lately.”

“And that’s okay,” Cara noted comfortably. “He’s his own person and will have his own unique spirit come and go throughout his lifetime.”

“What do you mean, come and go?”

“Sometimes, they check in and check out, depending on what their previous lifetimes have been.”

At that, everybody stopped.

Terk chuckled. “You’re pushing their belief systems again.”

She stared at him, frowning. “Are you telling me that you guys haven’t dealt with past lives?”

“No. We haven’t dealt with anything along that line at all.” Sophia stared at her in fascination.

Cara shrugged. “We tend to come back in groups,” she explained, “because we learn the best from those we love. Because nobody can hurt us in quite the same way as those we care about," she murmured. "Anyway I'm not saying that you've all been in past lives together. I'm just saying that children, if they'll release any information about their past life to you, will do so in the first four to six years. In most cases, they don't start until around the fourth year," she noted. "And that's because they haven't really had the necessary diction to even communicate at that level."

"That makes sense," Mariana noted, as Little Calum headed back to her.

Cara stood up, not sure she wanted to get into a heavy discussion on the subject. "I saw the commercial kitchen on my walkabout. Shall we go in and see about dinner?" She nodded to Rick, as she headed off. Mariana and Little Calum followed. "Rick, you want to set the table?"

He immediately headed toward a big box of cutlery in their kitchenette.

"Wow," Cara said. "You guys really haven't been here long, have you?"

"No." Mariana laughed. "Last trip out is when we picked up the extra cutlery and a bunch of the staples. We haven't had access to the big kitchen before, so we needed to get some basics."

"How did you manage to avoid detection or raising any alarms with that?" Cara asked curiously.

"We didn't actually. We knew the bad guys had spies who would likely be onto us, so we just stocked up and went for it. We did okay, until we stopped by my sublet apartment to try to get some of our things, hoping to avoid more stops. Yet going there triggered a response. Still we made it back in one piece, losing our tails. We bought a lot of food, though typically it would make sense to try to keep anyone from understanding how many we're trying to feed."

"Are you a cook?"

"She's a damn good chef," Cal said with pride, beaming at his wife and child, as he joined everyone.

"I am a caterer actually," she muttered, "but I haven't done a whole lot of work outside the home since Little Calum arrived. So I ran a business from my home, but not nearly what I did before."

"By choice?

"By choice, and my circumstances just changed," she said, looking over at Cal.

He walked closer, put an arm around her. "We're grateful to put your skills to use now."

She laughed. "That's just because, for you, it's all about your stomach."

"Not just for me," he replied, with mock humor. "Everybody here cares about their stomachs."

"I think we all do, no matter who we are," Cara agreed. "Especially in stressful times."

MARIANA SET ABOUT the work of cooking for the team in their big kitchen, and, by assigning tasks to her helpers, had a meal ready in no time. They all carried in dishes to the main room, setting up the food at the big table off the little kitchenette, yet near all their computers.

Everybody had arrived for dinner and were gathered around the table, when Cara looked at Tasha and Sophia. "Did you guys find anything about those alarms?"

Sophia nodded. "We had set an alarm up to see if anybody was searching for you. Unfortunately we got two hits." Sophia looked over at Terk. "We've got the names for you, but they're not likely to be the real names."

He nodded. "Not likely."

"And why would somebody be searching for me?" Cara asked.

"We wondered that ourselves, thinking their energy would be better served looking for any of the rest of us."

Cara shrugged. "I don't know what to say. What you guys are involved in is really none of my business."

"Unfortunately we did have to do some digging into your personal life," Tasha shared gently.

At that, Cara stiffened, and then slowly relaxed again. "Good thing I've led such a blameless life then, isn't it? Kind of a bore really."

"Well, you certainly have on paper," she murmured, "and there was no mention of your brother."

"Nope," she agreed. "He didn't make it."

After a moment of silence, Tasha continued. "I didn't find a death certificate."

"No, you won't," Cara noted smoothly. "He didn't die in the country of his birth, and he wouldn't necessarily make it through any efforts to transport him home." She looked over at Terk and shrugged. "That's up to you to discuss, if you want to."

"It's your brother," he said.

"It is, but, at the same time, nobody can do anything for him anymore."

"So how about we just get it all out in the open, so we're not all sitting here trying to figure out what you guys are talking about," Tasha suggested, a note of humor in her voice.

"I don't know about anybody else, but my mind is all over the place," Sophia admitted, with a chuckle.

Cara shrugged. "My brother was in the military, stationed in Iraq. When he got injured, he sent me a telepathic message. We've always been able to communicate, and I knew the moment he got hit. I desperately reached out, trying to find anybody who could help him. The only person who responded was Terk."

At that, all heads swiveled toward Terk.

She laughed. "But Terk was in, I think, China at the time." She frowned at him.

He nodded. "I think it was China, and we hadn't started this team yet."

"Anyway, we did get somebody out to my brother, but he didn't make it, and I stayed connected until he passed," she shared.

"So why is there no death certificate?" Rick asked.

"Because he was doing deep undercover work," she murmured. "He doesn't exist as far as the military is concerned. I know for a fact he's gone, but I didn't have a body to bury, and I don't need that particular closure because I was connected at the time of his death."

"I don't know too many families who could accept that," Lorelei noted softly.

"No, it can be hard," Cara agreed, "but I was connected, and we could speak with each other at the time. He knew that I loved him, and I did what I could to ease his pain, but I could do basically nothing else."

"So, why do you feel like you owe Terk?" Rick asked.

Terk waved a hand. "I've told her that she doesn't owe me anything."

"Because he connected with me," she murmured, "and, while Terk was busy trying to get somebody to come and physically help my brother, Terk also stayed connected to me, via his energy gifts. … And, until you actually stay connected to somebody who doesn't make it, you don't understand the loneliness and the pain of losing somebody that close to you," she explained, just barely holding back the choking in her voice.

She realized somebody was holding her hand. She looked down to see Rick's fingers wrapped around hers. She squeezed back gently.

"So, if there was something Terk needed me to do," she whispered, "I was there."

At that, another period of silence passed, as they all tried to assimilate what she had just said.

"And can you connect with other people or was it just your brother?"

"Well, once I realized that it wasn't just my brother, and it was also Terk," she admitted, "I did open myself up to an awful lot more people, and it's made a big difference to my patients." She paused. "Sometimes I can tell almost immediately that they're gone or that they're going or that they need to say goodbye, because the cord is mostly severed or disconnected or whatever." She shrugged. "It has helped immeasurably in my ability to communicate with those who may or may not be here."

"And so you thought that she could keep me alive? Is that right?" Rick asked Terk.

"I was hoping she could keep you alive and could help convince your subconscious self to come back to the land of the living," he murmured, "but I also knew that she wouldn't let you die alone. So, if we were to lose you, I didn't want to lose you in a way that meant I could never look myself in the face again."

It was a stunning announcement on Terk's part.

Rick sighed. "Ah, jeez. I feel like an ass." He rubbed at his face, trying to choose his words. "I've been incredibly ungrateful and angry because I felt like I was late getting here, late helping with all the stuff you guys were doing, and here you two were doing all that to keep me safe and sound, at least not to die alone."

She shrugged. "Obviously there's a whole lot more to energy healing. However, right now, I don't know about you guys, but I'm starving." She looked around at everyone. "Can we eat?"

Realizing it was a plea for separation from the subject, Mariana immediately called out, "Grab a plate, everyone. Come and get it while it's hot."

EVERYTHING CARA HAD explained was just so beautiful yet so far out there and so difficult to imagine that Rick didn't even know what to think. He waited until later in the evening, and then he caught Terk for a moment. "So I guess we need to find a way to get Cara safely back to her own life."

"You also need to realize"—Terk gazed at him—"that her own life has been one of helping people, patients, one way or another, cross over."

"Cross over?"

"Yes," he confirmed. "She made it sound like she's there to help them survive, and, if she can, she does, but, more often than not, she's helping them navigate death."

He winced at that. "Is that why you hired her for me?"

"Nope, I was pretty damn sure that you weren't ready to let go, and I just needed somebody to help convince you of that."

He smiled. "Well, you're right there. I'm definitely not. At the same time, I do feel like we need to get her back to her life."

"I hear you," Terk noted, "but it's just too dangerous right now. We'll have to find a way to do something though. Not tonight, not tomorrow, and probably not for a few days. I'd like to find out more about these people who have been searching for her."

"I presume it means that she was seen."

He nodded. "Probably outside when you left, before we picked you up."

"Too bad we couldn't have done that rescue inside a building," he murmured. "It would have kept her safer."

"Maybe," Terk agreed. "At the same time, it was also a chance that we had to take because we had to pick you up. Sounds like you got out of there in the nick of time."

"Yeah, we were about to be under attack, and I made her leave her clothes behind, but she had her purse with her. I didn't want to risk getting cornered in the apartment," he added.

"Got it, and I agree. It would have been nothing for them to have captured her face on one of their cameras and are now looking for her."

"And what will they find?" Rick asked him.

Terk gave him a lopsided look. "A whole lot less than they're expecting."

"Won't that set off alarms?"

"Probably, but there's not exactly a whole lot they can do about it." Terk shrugged. "Or us. She's very specialized, and she's very good at what she does."

"I get that," Rick noted, "and I really do owe her my life,

don't I?"

At that, Terk shrugged. "She wouldn't be happy to hear you using those terms, but the answer to that question is yes. She did an awful lot to keep you alive."

"Now we need to make sure we take care of her."

Terk looked over at Tasha. "Do we have anything to go on?"

"I'm backtracking them now," she stated.

"Honestly I believe we can clear her and get her out of our troubles," Terk stated, "but, yes, she and I both knew ahead of time that this scenario could be a problem."

"So then why did she do it?" Rick felt dazed.

"Because she cares," Terk stated. "One of the few people I know who comes from her heart in all ways."

Rick frowned at that, wondering if he should go find her, then realized Terk was talking to him. "Sorry, what?"

"I'll go run down two leads," he repeated. "Do you want to come?"

"Sure," Rick said. "Where are we going?"

"I want to see the two people who came to that apartment," Terk stated. "Our ITs identified who they are."

Rick stared at him in shock. "Hell, yes, I'm coming. I want to see who these assholes are."

"That's partly why I want to get you there. We also need to do a test on your abilities. So …" He let his voice trail off at that.

"Good enough," Rick noted. "I should—"

Terk shook his head. "Better if she doesn't know."

"I get that, but somehow I think she'll know anyway."

Terk laughed. "So true. While we're out"—he looked around at the rest of them—"do we need anything?"

"Always," Lorelei replied, with a smile. "Actually Mariana started a list. They got a lot the other day, but she added a few things."

He nodded. "Sounds good, and I haven't picked up anything in quite a while, so this is as good a time to go as any."

Rick hesitated at that. "Is it wise though, putting ourselves back out there again so soon?"

"That's one of the things we need to sort out. For us to see if they have any idea where we are, we have to make ourselves visible in order to catch them."

"They're already tracking Cara. Are they tracking me too?" Rick asked.

"I'm sure they're trying to," Terk noted, "but we scrubbed your identity from the internet as much as we could."

"But it'll never be completely scrubbed. What about the government database?" he asked.

"Well, that's what Lorelei was doing," Terk shared, with a smile.

At that, they walked out to the truck, and Terk drove out of the huge hangar attached to the warehouse space.

"This is quite the place," Rick noted. "I don't know what your plans are when this is all over with, but it would be hell on wheels if we could have a place like this to set up as a new base for the team."

"Funny you should say that," he said. "You're not the first person to mention setting up our own company."

"It'd be a good idea," Rick agreed.

"Although it's definitely a different atmosphere, having so many partners now, isn't it?" Terk asked.

"What about you?" Rick smirked. "When will you get one?"

At that question, there was an uneasy pause.

Rick looked over at his friend. "What did I say?"

"It's not what you said," he replied. "It's what I haven't filled you in on." And, with that, he quickly brought him up to date on the issue with Celia.

Rick stared in shock. "Oh, my God. How the hell could somebody know so much about us and hit us all in so many ways at the same time?"

"My only thought," Terk stated, "was the government."

Rick sank back in disgust. "Yeah, I know. That's how I felt." He turned toward Terk. "And yet nobody is talking?"

"No, though I've also been wondering if they subcontracted out the hit on our team."

"To somebody who really hates us?"

"Yeah, that would be the best bet, wouldn't it? Probably got a super price on the deal."

"Yet we haven't found anybody?"

"Not yet. We've looked back to Iran and the base that we took out, wondering whether or not it was that group."

"We took out everybody though."

"Did we? I mean, that's what they all thought about us, and here we still are."

"Good point," Rick murmured. "So who's left? I mean, and maybe it's not who's left, as much as what do they have for equipment or people in training who could be left."

"I don't know. We're still searching that avenue."

"And all these people you've been battling?"

"I think they've just been hired by the original core group to confirm that we actually died, and now that they're finding we didn't …"

"Now that they know we didn't, somebody is trying to clean up the mess left behind, and they're more than likely tweaking whatever it was that they did to take us out in the first place. If we were a trial run …"

"God," Terk interrupted. "That doesn't bear thinking about, and yet how can we not? And, if we were a trial run, how many other people are out there like us?"

"I didn't think there were very many at all," Rick admitted. "Cara was a complete shock to me."

"She is, and yet she isn't to me," he shared. "She has a lot of skill, and she had that all on her own. She developed it by her desire and willingness to help others. So the skills that she has are much more defined than we expect to see in the general population."

"But that still doesn't mean a lot of people like us are out there."

"Well, we did find the Iran group, who were just like us, doing energy work," he added.

"So," Rick added, "it only makes sense that, if we found them, some other people did too."

Terk nodded. "That was my thought."

As they kept driving, Rick looked around at the city. "Do you have a place in mind?"

"Yes," he said. "I need to go pick up weapons."

He stiffened at that. "What are we doing for money?"

"Well, let me just say that I was able to make some changes to a certain bank account, when I realized what was going on."

"Oh, my gosh." Rick stared at Terk, and then Rick started to laugh and laugh. "That was brilliant. Talk about turning the tables on them."

"Well, they just lost all the money that was in our expense account," Terk noted, "and, of course, I'm sure you understand that Merk and company have been helping us."

"Of course they have," Rick said. "I'm surprised I haven't seen him."

"Oh, he's around," Terk confirmed. "He was there when we picked you up too. It's part of the reason we know who was tracking you because he followed them back to their base."

"Is that where we're going?" he asked eagerly.

He nodded. "But just for reconnaissance."

"Ah." Rick nodded. "So you want to do some searching, and I'm here to help you ground."

"Something like that," he agreed. "Actually Cal is hoping to connect with me while we're here, as a test to see how we're doing."

"Interesting," Rick murmured. "Just like old times. All part of our training."

"Yes." Terk nodded.

Rick added, "I had hoped we were well past all that training."

"Never," Terk replied seriously. "Never. I think it's something that we always have to do to keep up our abilities."

"Right," Rick agreed. "It's just not the way we wanted to have to do it."

"No, it isn't, but that's okay. Once we're all up to speed again," Terk shared, "we'll be a really strong unit."

As they drove farther to whatever destination Terk had in mind, Rick looked at him. "Have you put any thought into a team after this?"

"I haven't," he said, "not at this point in time. Maybe, when we get this all sorted out, we'll see."

"Well, I'll just bet that everybody will want to have answers in place before that."

Terk laughed. "That would make a lot of sense too.

You're right. They are all going to want answers pretty damn fast."

"So, why don't you start thinking about it now, and see what you can give us for answers?"

Terk shook his head. "I also have to sort out the Celia situation, and I don't have a clue what that'll look like."

"I get it. Cara filled me on that," Rick noted. "I really do. I can't even imagine Cal walking away from his wife and his son."

"In his mind, he didn't so much walk away as remove the hazard. He believed that, if he stayed away from them, they would be safe. He has supported them financially, so Mariana didn't have to work, unless she wanted to, and his plan had been to reunite, after this retirement of ours."

"I'm glad to hear that," Rick said. "Did you see any of this coming?"

Terk frowned. "No, and believe me. That's one thing that I'm really struggling with."

"You're a seer, but even you can't see everything."

"I should have seen this. I should have seen what was coming for all of us." He slammed his hand against the steering wheel. "This is beyond devastating in my world. There should have been a sign, multiple signs. There should have been something to tip me off that this was happening, but there wasn't."

"And how much of that," Rick suggested, "is because of your own senses being dulled by whatever our attackers did?"

"I should have seen it anyway, before the attack," he murmured. "Talk about a crisis of conscience and abilities and questioning everything I've ever done. I mean, what's the point of having all these so-called abilities, if we can't even utilize them to save ourselves?" he murmured.

"I don't know," Rick admitted. "You've often saved Merk and his family and that whole company, so it's odd that you didn't get any warning about us."

"I know. Believe me. I know. And yet I don't know why, but one of these days I will find out. However, I don't know what it is right now, and, until then," he said, "I'm not sure that I'm any good as a leader. To take on setting up as a private company and to do this all over again?" He shook his head. "What for? If I can't even save us, who is it I'm trying to save?"

They reached their destination faster than Rick expected. When Terk shut off the engine, he sat here for a long few minutes.

"You want to explain how you want to play this?" Rick asked him.

"I want Cal to step in and see if he can find anything while remote reviewing."

"But he needs a destination, doesn't he?"

"Yes, in which case, that's something we'll get him."

"And how will we do that?" Rick asked, looking at Terk.

"Well, hopefully," Terk said, "we'll go in and take a look."

Rick shook his head. "That doesn't sound like a normal operation."

"Nothing about this is normal anymore. My brother says two are here, and he's here right now, as well."

Just then came a shadow at the driver's side door.

Terk opened it. "Hey, Merk. Look who I brought."

"Who?" Merk leaned in. "Good to see you alive, man."

"Yeah," Rick replied, with feeling. "Nice to be alive too."

Merk smiled. "Hey, the more of you who come back online, the better the world'll be."

"I don't know about that," Rick said. "I'm still feeling—it's just good to be back."

"Yeah, but you're still not feeling up to snuff."

"I'm not doing too badly," he said cautiously. "Still getting my strength back." He jerked. In fact, he was feeling a little different. He didn't know what the hell that was, and he looked over at Terk. "Something feels off."

Terk nodded. "And I can't help you with that. You'll have to sort it out."

"*Great*," he muttered. "So is Cal ready to do some viewing?"

Terk pulled out his phone, sent a text, and got a reply right back. "Yes, he's ready."

Merk shook his head. "Hell of a system. Sometimes you guys talk telepathically, and other times you need phones? I don't get it."

"Telepathic communication takes energy," Terk explained. "And, right now, I need Cal to take a look inside and see just who's in there and who's not."

"I told you that I saw two go in," Merk repeated.

"Yeah, I heard you," Terk confirmed. "What I need to know is if more are in there or not."

"Got it, and how will you do that?" Merk asked, with half a smile.

At that, Terk grinned. "Just watch and see, watch and see." He turned to Rick. "Ready?"

Rick took a deep breath. "Sure, let's do this."

And Rick closed his eyes, searched out Cal's energy, as Rick set up a grounding station for Cal. Almost immediately, Rick felt Cal surging his energy up and around Rick. It felt good. It felt normal. It felt whole. Rick smiled to see that he had almost no side effects to being back in this old position again. He almost reveled in it.

There was such a sense of power all around him. He couldn't do a whole lot while he was charging the energy, but, as long as he could charge, he was doing his job. When the energy was cut off a few minutes later, he opened his eyes and looked over at Terk. "Did he get what he needed?" he asked.

"He did, and he didn't," Terk replied.

Just then Terk's phone rang. Cal was put on Speaker. "Hey, Rick. What happened?"

"What do you mean, what happened?"

"That's what I want to know. Everything was great, and then, all of a sudden, it just stopped."

At that, Terk's lips twitched. "I have an idea about what happened, but I don't know for sure. Rick, it wasn't you, was it?"

"No, not me," he stated, "and you're right. It felt normal, great actually. I felt like I could get in there and just do what I needed to do."

Cal said, "Shit. I'm pissed that happened. Can we try it again? Maybe we'll have better results."

"You can," Terk said. "Give us a minute though. I'll send you a text when we're ready."

"Good enough," Cal replied.

Terk hung up, and Rick looked over at his boss and friend. "What the hell is going on?"

"I'm pretty sure that somebody put a governor on your energy."

Rick stared at him in shock. "What? Like a governor on a car or something?"

"Or *something*," Terk repeated, with a smirk.

At that comment, Rick stared. "Cara can't do that, can

she?"

Terk's lips twitched again. "Maybe you should assess your own energy and let me know."

At that, Rick closed his eyes and checked out his energy. "Good Lord, how can she be that strong?"

"She wouldn't think anything of it, but, in her mind, she would say that you hit a dangerous point in your healing, and she just shut it off."

Merk looked at Rick, then Terk, and asked, "*She?*"

Terk explained, "Remember how I brought Cara in to help Rick?"

"I do remember that. She's got that kind of ability?" Merk asked in awe.

Terk nodded. "Yes, it's one of the reasons Rick's still alive because she's making sure that he is. She's guarding his energy and keeping him safe."

"Well, she can't just keep doing that," Rick snapped. "I needed that power."

"She just didn't understand what you were doing with it," Terk noted. "You haven't talked to her about any of this, have you?"

"Some, but not this part," he admitted. "Everything has always been top secret, you know? That we don't discuss with anyone but each other."

"I get that," Terk agreed, "but I think, before you try again, we must have a talk with her and let her know that this is normal stuff and that this is what you do."

Rick was still stunned, when he realized that Terk was actually serious. "You really think she stopped me?"

"I'm pretty damn sure she did," Terk stated. "Close your eyes and power up again and see what you get."

Immediately he shut his eyes and worked to power up

some of that same energy, using Terk's to come back online, but nothing was there. Finally, in frustration, he opened his eyes, stared at Terk, and nodded. "I think you're right. I think she shut me down." He stared at Merk, who was now laughing uproariously. "It's hardly funny," Rick snapped.

"The hell it's not," Merk argued. "It's beyond funny. Here you guys are the pros in all this, doing your best to save the world, and a single woman comes in, and, just like that, she shuts off your source of power. Jesus." Merk's face was red from his chortling. "I haven't seen something so funny in quite a while." And, with that, he went off belly-laughing again.

Terk looked over at the furious Rick, gave him half a smile. "You can hardly blame her."

"Why the hell not?" he snapped. "This is beyond anything I've ever seen before."

"Sure, but so is she," Terk added. "Why do you think I tried to recruit her?"

"Well, at least then she would understand where her role starts and stops."

"Sure, but remember. You also allowed her to do that."

He stared at him. "What do you mean?"

"Remember the first law of energy? You have *allowed* her to do this."

"Like hell I did," Rick retorted hotly.

"Before, she was saving you, when you needed that help," Terk explained. "And you probably weren't in any condition to fight it, but now you're stronger, and you're the one who needs to put some boundaries in place. But, like I said, you must do it in the proper way. Otherwise you'll just piss her off."

"Are you thinking she'd stop me or be a danger to me

somehow?" Rick asked. "Is that what you're saying?"

"No," Terk stated. "It's something infinitely more valuable, but you'll have to figure that out for yourself." And, with that, Terk sighed. "Now, experiment completed. Better let Cal know we're done. We'll do these errands, then head home."

CHAPTER 6

CARA OPENED HER eyes, startled at a weird sensation going on in her brain. She immediately sat up, walked around her room, frowning. When her phone rang, she looked at her screen. It was Rick. She answered it. "Hello?"

"I'm not sure what's going on," he began, his tone very careful, "but you do understand that I need energy, right?"

She frowned at the phone. "I don't know what you're talking about," she replied caustically, "and if you're accusing me of something, I suggest you just back off right there. All I'm trying to do is get home. I don't know what your problem is."

"Yeah, see? I'm not so sure," he said, "if you're doing this on purpose or if you're doing it subconsciously."

She stared at the phone in surprise, but a moment of awareness clicked in the back of her head. "You want to explain what you're talking about?"

"Or you could," he suggested carefully. "We're at a site, and we were trying to test my abilities."

"Look. I don't know what you're implying," she stated stiffly, "but I don't appreciate that note of accusation in your voice." She heard him take a slow breath, as if reaching for control.

"I get that, in your world, you have been working to keep me safe," he murmured. "But, right now, I also need to stretch a bit and see what I'm capable of doing."

"And?" she asked in a stiff voice.

He sighed. "Maybe you're not even doing it consciously. I don't know, but it appears to me that you've put, for lack of a better word, a governor of sorts on my abilities."

She stopped for a moment, then smiled. "I see."

"Does that make sense?"

"If you're asking whether I have been limiting your ability to do things on an energy level, then yes," she admitted. "I have been."

"Well, could you please stop it?" he growled.

At that, she realized just how much it was affecting him to know that she could do it to begin with and that now he was in the position of having to ask her to stop.

"Yes, I think I could do that." She kept her voice as stiff as his was because it was hardly a topic of discussion she wanted to have over the phone. "It is there for your protection, however."

"I understand and appreciate that. Yet I'm no longer unconscious and don't need that level of protection," he argued carefully.

She sniffed. "Says you." And, with that, she hung up.

She glared down at the phone but realized that it would have happened at some point in time anyway. Normally she took that level of control off much earlier, but things had happened so fast with their change of venue that she hadn't really had a chance to assess where his levels were at. She sat down on the bed and mentally removed several of the blocks around his energy.

When she received a smile through her mind, she realized it was Terk. She sent him back a blank response. She wasn't ready to talk to him either. He's the one who had gotten her into this mess, and, although she'd come willing-ly, she was in a situation right now that she certainly wasn't comfortable with—obviously neither was Rick, but that was his own fault.

He's the one who was in this scenario, and all she was trying to do was keep him safe. Obviously she should have pulled that *governor* back off a little bit earlier, but how was she supposed to know what he was doing out there? It's not like he'd told her, and, then again, she'd never told him that she had his energy in check either. Maybe it would be good for him to find out firsthand that he wasn't doing as well as he thought he was. She pondered that for a moment and then nodded and removed all the energy blocks and energy lines to his system and let him go free.

"Take that," she muttered. "Maybe you're fine, and maybe you're not. At least this will help you determine where you're at."

And, with that, she walked back out to the main room, still a little on the disgruntled side, and made herself a cup of tea. As it was, most of the others were gone. She found Mariana with Little Calum at the dining table, having popcorn. Cara looked at the popcorn and smiled. "Talk about something that makes you feel like a touch of home."

"Would you like some?" Mariana asked.

She shook her head. "No thanks, I'm fine," she mur-mured. "I hadn't realized the guys were out on a job."

"I'm not sure what they're doing," Mariana admitted. "Cal's still here, but he's involved somehow, holed up in one of Terk's rooms. I think, around here, the team doesn't always communicate well with the others."

"Well, I think they'd all benefit from more communica-tion," Cara stated.

"I agree. I'm just not sure that they're used to explaining themselves."

She laughed at that. "No, I don't think they are, and I won't be here long enough for it to become an issue. At least I hope not."

At that, Mariana looked over at her. "Are you sure?" she asked in a gentle voice.

Cara frowned. "What does that mean?"

"It's obvious that you're very connected to Rick in some way."

"Sure." Cara nodded. "It's part of the healing process, but I'm working on disconnecting that energy now."

There must have been something in her voice that showed some of her disgruntlement. At that, Mariana looked at her intently. "Is something wrong?"

"No, not necessarily." Cara shrugged. "It's always hard when you let go of a patient you've been working with and trying to keep safe, especially when you don't know if he's quite ready or safe to be on his own."

"Well, with these guys, I think they're, … I don't want to say, *superhuman*," she added, "because obviously that's incorrect, since they are very much normal human beings in that they can get hurt, just as much as the rest of us." She raised one eyebrow and gave a tilt of her head. "But I think it's fascinating to note that they do have the ability to heal quite quickly."

"They do, but it also takes effort on the part of the others to make it happen," Cara argued. "In Rick's case, he's not healed, and he was pushing the envelope already, and—of course, right now—he's pushing it even further."

"Of course," Mariana agreed. "Can you tell if he'll go down? You know, like with a power outage?"

"I don't even know how to say it either." Cara laughed. "I mean, I get that all kinds of issues surround the team. I'm just trying to figure it out."

"But are you connected enough that you can tell when Rick's in trouble?"

"Not any longer, … at least I don't think so." She frowned. "I was connected, and he just called me and basically told me to terminate it."

At that, Mariana looked at her and then started to chuckle. "Well, that explains the look on your face."

Cara shrugged. "It's weird. I mean, up until just a few hours ago, I was looking after him, and apparently now he's looking after himself." She shook her head. "Of course that's what we want, to have everybody back on their feet and functioning in this way. It's just a weird, very quick shift that I'm not accustomed to."

"These guys do move very quickly, and when you least expect it," Mariana noted. "So I wouldn't take it personally."

"It's hard after being connected to him for all this time."

Mariana nodded solemnly. "And that's a good point. Your healing ability is something we haven't all had the advantage of, you know?"

Cara shrugged. "I don't even know how much of a healing ability it was, but he's on his own now."

"Maybe that's what he needs, so he can figure out whether he's strong enough to go or not?"

"That's what I figured," Cara replied, "so I cut him loose. We'll see how he does."

It wasn't too long before they heard the sounds of someone returning. Cara felt herself stiffen. "You know what? I really don't want to deal with them tonight." She smiled at Mariana. "So I'll be in my room." And, with that, she got up to leave.

"Don't run away though," Mariana warned.

Cara stopped and stared at her. "Is that what I'm doing?"

"Of course it is, and I get it. Believe me. I do. I've had plenty of issues of my own with Cal," she murmured. "And, until we were kidnapped, he was trying to keep me at a distance too."

"Is that what Rick's doing?" she asked, intently staring at her. "I'm not really good at leaving a patient at the end. I tend to get quite cranky. Honestly, when I go from full control to zero control," she added, "it's an adjustment that I don't make very well."

Mariana smiled. "And maybe, in this case, it's someone who you've also given your heart to. So, when you and your skills are no longer needed, it feels like a rejection."

She thought about it and nodded. "Maybe so, but I've dealt with a lot of patients. It shouldn't be affecting me like this."

"Did you do anything different in this case?"

She frowned and then winced. "Maybe. I have done it a few other times, but mostly when it's already been too late, and I've lost the patient."

"So this time you did something that you've done before, but this time it worked?" she asked.

"Yes."

"So, that's created a very strong bond."

"Yeah, maybe so, and that'll cause me more problems than I'm really looking for," she murmured. She shook her head. "I knew at the time it was a possibility. I just didn't realize how bad it would be."

"I'm sorry," Mariana said. "That is a problem."

"It is, indeed, but whatever." Cara looked up, as she heard more sounds of the men coming back in. "It's definitely them, so I'll leave you on your own."

She turned and quickly headed back to her room. She had just closed the door when the men walked into the inner sanctum. She heard Rick ask where she was. She couldn't hear the answer that Mariana gave but figured she'd probably say that Cara had just left. She immediately walked into the bathroom and turned on the shower water, so she wouldn't have to deal with him knocking on her door.

If there was ever anything she didn't want to deal with right now, it was him. She had her own chaotic emotions to get control of. He was right. If he was strong enough, then she had no business putting any control over his energy. But how was she supposed to have known that he was strong enough or that he would be out testing it?

Hell, he didn't even know if he was strong enough here, so why would he be going off-site to test it? And it's not like he even told her. She went ahead and took a quick shower and dressed in her pajamas, thankful that Merk had at least gotten her bags from her apartment, grateful to have something with her now, so she wasn't so completely dependent on these guys.

It was time that she started to make some plans, in her head at least. She didn't know how long it would take to get out of here, but it was even more important now for her to leave. Her heart was way too involved, and it would take her time and a lot of pain to separate, and that was something she did not want to do when Rick was around.

It would hurt enough as it was, and the last thing she wanted to do was to have the whole group watching her pain of separation. She'd always been a private person, and that hadn't changed. The work she did was usually one on one, and that made it a little bit easier when it came to this stage. Most of the time she could rejoice in a family reclaiming a child who had been badly injured, and Cara could leave happy.

In this case, it was a whole different story, and she didn't like it; she didn't like it at all. When she finally left the bathroom to return to her bedroom, she stopped. Rick stood there, waiting for her. She raised an eyebrow. "What's the matter? You don't knock?"

"I did knock," he stated, unperturbed at her tone.

She glared at him. "Well, if you're here to give me more shit, forget it. I'm not in the mood."

"Look. I didn't mean to be harsh," he began and then stopped.

"Sure you did," she snapped. "You wanted something. You got it. Now you can leave."

"No, I'm not planning on leaving. Not until we sort this out."

"There's nothing to sort out," she argued. "You were sick. I did my job. You think you're fine now. I pulled back. Whatever else you seem to think that I might have done, you're wrong. You're completely on your own. Absolutely nothing to fuss about." She stopped then and looked at him. "Did you find the bad guys?"

He shook his head. "No. We're going back with a bigger team."

"Well, that's good. Maybe you won't be so hell-bent on being Rambo."

He stared at her for a moment. "Do you really think I'm not capable of doing whatever it is I'm trying to do?"

"I don't know if you are or not," she stated flatly. "You

haven't been, and that's all I have to go by."

He nodded. "I get that. I really do, but I have to be able to function."

"Good. Why are you still here then? Go. Go off and do your little Rambo thing."

He frowned at her, as again, she just gave him a flat stare. The last thing she wanted to be having was this conversation. "Go." She waved her hands at him. "I'm going to bed. Get lost."

He started to laugh. "That's not the normal response I get from women," he noted in a cheeky voice.

At that, she turned and glared at him. "Well, maybe it's time you did. I'm tired, and I need to go to bed."

He nodded slowly. "You know that I really do appreciate everything you've done."

She held up her hand. "Stop. That is the last thing I want to hear. Just go. Get lost."

Frowning, he reluctantly walked over toward the door. "I really wasn't expecting that you could even do something like that."

"You don't know anything about me. So why would you?"

"What if I wanted to?"

"Well, it wouldn't work," she replied immediately.

He stared at her. "You went to a lot of effort to save my life."

"I owe Terk," she stated flatly. She refused to give an inch on anything. Inside her heart was already struggling, and the last thing she needed was to have more emotional crap flowing through him to her. He didn't understand, and maybe it was best that way. "I'll be fine. Don't worry."

"Yes, but I wouldn't want anything to happen to you,

particularly if it's because of what you did to me to help me out."

"Like I said, it's not your problem now. Go. Your friends are waiting for you. You need to set up a plan and do your stuff."

He frowned, as he looked back at the other room. "Do you actually know that they're waiting for me or was that just a guess?"

"What? You think now I can read your mind? Or am I just going to sit here, and you're worried about what I can do?"

"Of course I'm worried about what you can do," Rick admitted. "I've never seen anything like that before. My energy just completely shut off, like somebody turned off the tap."

"It was a tap. You wanted me to take the tap governor off, so I did. Does that make a difference to you? You probably don't feel that somebody else should be able to control you, but what you keep forgetting in all of this is," she said, "whether you actually know what level of energy to use that is safe for you? When I put that tap on, any excess usage past that definitely wasn't safe."

She turned to face him. "Based on the fact that you're still standing here in front of me, not singed or blown up, I presume you didn't get any further with your next attempt either."

He slowly shook his head. "No, I didn't."

THE NEXT MORNING Rick finally approached Terk about it. Rick had still been trying to wrap his mind around what had happened with Cara's tap, and it just seemed like he was not getting the full picture, was making a big deal out of nothing, or this really was a big deal, and he just didn't know how to handle it.

Terk asked him, "You still seem to be pretty shook up."

"Amazed, terrified, worried, exasperated, joyful—pretty much all of the above," Rick said instantly. "I've been thinking about it all night." He explained what Cara had said last night, when he'd asked her about it. Then somehow she knew that he had tried to ground energy again, and it didn't work, as Terk already knew.

Terk nodded slowly. "And you think that she lied, and she didn't actually remove all the controls?"

"I don't know that," he admitted quietly. "I mean, I want to believe her."

"I suggest you do," Terk noted, "but I can understand why you would be hesitant."

He threw up his hands. "I mean, all of this is so far-fetched."

"Well, you didn't have a problem believing in your abilities before, so what do you think happened?"

"I'm not sure," he said. "I'm really not sure. I mean, I know that I'm a bit weak and not up to full strength, but I was expecting to have more than what I did."

"And because she had the governor on, you're still afraid that that's the reason, right?"

"Well, it's a reasonable hypothesis," he tried to explain.

"It is, indeed." Terk nodded. "So maybe you need to talk to her again."

"No, that I don't need to do. I got raked over the coals pretty good the last time."

Terk laughed. "You might want to consider the situation

from her perspective. She was doing what she thought was right, to protect you, and you slapped her down."

He just gave him a flat stare at that. "I get that, but, as long as she doesn't do it again, it's not a problem."

"But if she does do it again?"

He nodded. "That's a big problem for me. The fact that she even is capable of doing something like that just blows me away. It makes me not want to sleep at night because I just don't understand, and I don't know how much control she might still have."

"If she has any, you mean," he reminded him.

"Exactly. If she has any. She tells me that she has removed all ability to do that, but that doesn't mean she can't put it right back on."

"What she did was for your own healing, so don't think of her as having done something against your will or anything else," Terk reminded him. "She was the primary force keeping you alive, and now that you obviously have made it clear to her that you don't need that from her anymore, she's probably still trying to figure out what she is doing next."

"I know she wants to leave," he said instantly.

"And I'm afraid it won't be quite that easy. We haven't solved our problems yet, in order to make sure that she can safely leave."

"And that's another problem. It's weird." He stopped, shrugged. "I don't know. I don't even know what I'm saying."

"Well, maybe you should continue, so I can understand it," Terk suggested.

"It's like there's a weird connection."

"Of course there is," he agreed instantly.

"Well, like she told me last night—to go visit with everybody in the computer room and to make plans—as if she already knew ahead of time what everybody was doing."

"Ah. So now you're thinking that she can read minds?"

"We've certainly seen that ability before. You have that ability to a certain extent," Rick noted. "I've just never come across it like this."

"Like this, or when it affected you?"

"Both," Rick agreed. "I'm not trying to make a big deal out of this, but somehow it appears to be a big deal, and I don't know how I feel about it."

"Well, maybe you should get clear about that fact first," Terk noted, "because I don't think you're thinking very clearly on all the aspects involved. One, she's not doing anything to harm you. Two, she has done a lot to heal you. Three, everything she currently might be doing or thinking is still about whether it's safe for you to be on your own."

"Am I really that bad off?" he asked in amazement.

"It's quite possible," Terk noted. "I haven't really assessed your energy. I haven't had time, honestly. However, if she kept that governor on, I'll presume it's because she felt there was a need."

He nodded. "I get it. I absolutely do. It's just a really weird space to be in right now."

"Hold off on the judgment," Terk suggested, "and maybe work on that whole acceptance and forgiveness and gratitude thing, and see where you end up in a few days."

"Will she be here in a few days?" he asked, staring at his friend.

"I don't know. Can we get her out of here safely? I think we need to solve whoever was going into that apartment and tracking the two of you first," Terk stated. "Then she can go back to her life."

"I'm hearing a *maybe* in there."

"Sure, it's a maybe," Terk confirmed. "I hadn't really considered that her life would be in danger at the time, though honestly it probably wouldn't have stopped me because I was desperately trying to keep you all alive and really needed the help," he shared. "But I would not be happy if she became a casualty of that."

"Neither would I," Rick said instantly. "Jesus. I would not want that to happen at all. She has given up a large portion of whatever was going on in her world to help me, so let's not allow Cara to be part of our crap."

"It would be nice if we could keep it separate," Terk noted, "but I'm not sure how we can do that."

He sighed. "Fine. I won't get too upset, and I'll try not to be too worried about it all."

"Yet you will," Terk stated. "Just don't go overboard."

EARLY IN THE morning, Rick joined the gathering group, eating breakfast and making plans to go back to the house, where they had tracked the guys who found Rick and Cara at the apartment earlier. He looked over at Terk. "Do we know if they are still there?"

Tasha answered that question. "According to the satellite images, nobody has been in or out."

"Okay," Rick said, "then we need to go in and take a look, and I want to be in on it." His voice was harder than necessary.

Terk looked at him and frowned. "I'm not sure you're ready."

"I'm not either, but there's only one way to find out," he stated.

Terk gave him a flat stare.

And then Rick realized what the problem really was. He was also supposed to be part of a team, and here he was, just worried about himself. His shoulders sagged. "Sorry. I'm just anxious to not be seen as *less than*."

At that, Tasha and Sophia started to laugh.

"Oh, my God, you guys," Tasha said. "Enough already. We've heard that from every single one of you who have slowly gotten back on your feet. Some are pretty much back to normal, if they get enough rest, and some are still fighting us on it, but you'd never know because they're trying to hide it."

"Sure," Rick muttered. "None of us want to be in this situation."

"Of course not," Tasha agreed. "None of you do, but, if you all would set aside your egos, you'd find out that you've all basically been in the same boat."

Rick sat back, frowning. "Good to know, but I would still like to give it a good test and see what I can do." Although letting everyone down if he failed was not a good move.

Just then, as if on cue, the door opened, and Cara joined them. "Good morning." She walked over to the coffeepot and poured herself a cup.

Rick sensed the unease in his own energy and yet he felt a sense of rightness to it, as she approached. She sat down beside him but didn't say anything. He was grateful that she wasn't avoiding him, and he was surprised where she chose to sit. They had such an odd relationship between them right now. It was still very much a healer-patient thing, which added to the complexity, but also something else was there, that he didn't even begin to know how to understand.

As soon as breakfast was over, he stood and glanced around at the rest of the team in the room. "Terk and I will head out. Stand watch, will you?"

Immediately they all nodded.

"We've got your back," Sophia noted calmly. "Just don't do anything stupid."

At that, Rick felt Cara stiffen beside him. Rick looked at her reassuringly. "I promise that I won't do anything stupid." She just gave him a flat stare, and he knew she didn't believe him. He sighed. "Honest. I'm not an idiot."

Reluctantly she nodded. "Good. Then you shouldn't have any problems."

Even that was more than he expected, more than he'd hoped for, and he was grateful for at least that vote of confidence from somebody who actually knew the condition he was in. With that, he gave her a bright smile. "Thank you." He turned and exited the building.

As soon as he got outside, he froze, hesitating. When Terk came up beside him, Rick asked, "Why is it I feel like I can't leave?"

"You tell me." Terk seemed curious. "Are you picking up something?"

"Well, something, but I don't know what. It's the darndest thing."

"Maybe what you're picking up is something more like an emotion."

He looked over at him. "Like?"

Terk smiled. "Did you say goodbye to somebody?" His voice was so soft and so supportive that it took Rick a moment to realize.

"Oh, boy. Is that what's going on?"

"You tell me," Terk said, a note of amusement in his voice. "You're the one feeling whatever you're feeling. It's up to you to tell the rest of us."

And his heart sank. "But she already knows, doesn't she?"

Terk looked at Rick, his lips twitching. "What do you think?" Terk asked Rick.

"Shit." Rick sagged in place. "I don't know what to do about that."

"Why don't you do nothing for the moment," Terk suggested calmly, "and just see. Maybe it'll change now that she has separated the energy."

"Yeah. Something has changed, and I feel like I pulled the wings off a butterfly or something."

At that, Terk started to laugh.

"I'm not sure she'd like that reference either," Rick admitted. "Does this happen to her every time?"

"Sometimes," Terk noted, "but, don't forget. Usually at the level that she went to, in order to keep you alive, she lost most of them."

And then it hit him. How would that play out over time with Cara, again and again, the depths of that connection she had with each of her critically ill patients and the pain of disconnecting? "Good God," he whispered. "How could she do that over and over again?"

"I think mostly because she believes she has a calling for it, and there was a need."

"What about the ones she did heal?"

"I think she had a way of separating from them, and it could be just as simple as knowing that her patients were going to be with somebody else. The other thing is …" Terk hesitated.

"Don't stop now." Rick stared at Terk. "If you know anything, I need to hear it."

"I know a lot about her gifts," Terk agreed, "but I don't know her exact process—what she had to do to keep you alive. I just know that it was a huge investment of time and energy. She did it willingly, but there'll be a payoff for that, you know? And, in this case, more than a payoff, maybe a price."

"Well, she had to separate."

"And you made it very clear that you wanted it done … and not necessarily in an easy way. So, from her perspective, she may be feeling like she's been abandoned. Psychologically she knows how this will play out, so no wonder she wants to leave right away."

"And just the thought of her leaving makes me sick," Rick murmured.

Terk smiled. "Yeah, and that's the thing. It's a two-way street."

"So, what you're saying is, whether I like it or not, we're bonded?"

"What I'm saying is," Terk stated, "this was a byproduct of healing you. And, yes, it happened without your prior permission. Yes, you're bonded. Now the question is, what will you do about it?"

CHAPTER 7

ONE THING ABOUT knowing where Rick stood, it meant Cara needed to pick up and to start fresh somewhere else. She'd had similar emotions many times over, and it always came back to her patients. She was happy that they were doing so well, but it also left her in an odd state. This time with Rick was way worse and was her own fault.

She shouldn't have taken on something this dark. Honestly she hadn't been sure that he would make it. Yet, when she'd seen that little tiny bit of hope, she'd dove in as hard and as fast as she could to save him. However, the penalty for that was how she was the one who would hurt.

Rick just wanted to move on and to get back to his old life, and she couldn't blame him for that. She couldn't blame him for any of this. It was her fault; she needed to take responsibility for that. When she went out to the main room, she asked calmly, "Is there a laptop here I can use?"

Tasha looked at her and asked, "Did nobody get you yours?"

"Is it here?" she asked in delight.

Tasha nodded and walked over to where a stack of electronics sat. "Do you need a mouse with that?"

"There should have been one with it," Cara noted. They rummaged around until she found it. "Perfect." Looking around at the three women, all at the three computer stations, Cara said, "I'll just take this back into my room then."

"Or," Sophia offered, "you can set up over here, if you want."

Cara hesitated and then shrugged. "Sure, if you don't mind. I don't really want to spend all my time in my room."

"And you don't have to," Tasha stated immediately. "You're more than welcome to be out here with us."

She smiled. "Thank you for that. I feel like I'm here on sufferance."

"Not at all," Tasha noted warmly. "You don't have to earn your way here by any means. Anybody who worked as hard as you did to care for Rick is more than welcome here, anytime and all the time," she stated firmly. "And listen. Just because he's caught up in his own mess of emotions right now, that doesn't mean you have to be as well."

She laughed. "I'm afraid it's part of the job description."

"I don't know how you do it," Sophia shared. "Particularly if the patients die."

"Honestly, sometimes death is easier than those who are caught somewhere in between."

The women looked at her, fascinated. "We'll need to talk more about that sometime," Tasha noted. "But now we need to be watching the satellite feed to make sure nobody leaves that house before our guys get there."

"Are these guys in that house the same guys who they think were hunting us?"

"Yes. Well, we don't know that for sure, but we tracked them here via Merk, then confirmed via satellite. Yet, so far, every time we get to one of these places, we find more bodies than anything."

Cara looked at her in surprise, then at the satellite image

on the computer screen. "Are you saying that is the house in question?"

They nodded.

"Well, I can tell you right now that nobody's in that house."

"We can see two bodies," Tasha corrected her.

"Yes, you may have two *bodies*, but you don't have any live people. They're dead."

Sophia looked at her in shock. "How can you tell?"

"Because I see energy," she replied. "I'm not opening myself up to feel it, but I can tell you that nobody's there. I'm not sure how long they may have been there"—she frowned—"but they haven't been dead all that long."

"No, they can't have been because we're still getting infrared readings, saying some heat's there."

"Yeah, but it can take a while for the bodies to cool down, particularly if they've turned up the heat in the house," Cara noted calmly.

Tasha nodded. "Yes, I've seen that too."

"Ouch," Sophia said from beside Cara.

"Is anybody ever ready to say goodbye?" Mariana asked quietly, having just joined them. "I mean, if it were my son, I don't think I could handle it."

Cara looked at her and smiled., "You know what? That's often part of the problem, particularly with children. They aren't necessarily ready to say goodbye."

"And yet you seem to be okay with it?"

"No, kicking and screaming is the way I go all the time," Cara admitted. "So, when it does come to goodbyes, I do have more experience than others. And, if it's a death, I'm actually better with that because I know that they're going someplace safe."

And again, the women turned and looked at her in fascination.

Cara shrugged. "Anyway, you might want to tell the guys something's off with that whole scenario."

"What do you mean by *off*?" Tasha asked, immediately pulling up her phone. "Can you give me a little bit more than that?"

"Can't you talk to Rick? Tell him yourself," Sophia suggested.

"In order to separate and to not become a basket case," Cara explained, "I've shut all doors."

"Does that mean you can't communicate with him?" Tasha asked.

"Not without opening doors," Cara explained, "and then I'd be overwhelmed."

"Right, I won't pretend that I absolutely understand what you're saying," Mariana added, "but I do understand about that connection and the pain of losing somebody. I've always had a connection with Cal. So, when he went down, Terk contacted me," she murmured. "I didn't think I would survive it. If I hadn't had Little Calum to care for, I would have been totally fixated on Cal."

"I understand. It's hard," Cara agreed. "When you love, you love deep."

Mariana looked at her, smiling. "And that's a good way to be."

"Is it?" Cara gave her half a smile. "Sometimes it just feels like it's way more torture than it's worth."

"Now that you two are together, you should be fine," Mariana noted. "The pain comes from all the uncertainty."

And again, all eyes stared at Cara.

She shrugged. "I deal with people dying all the time, and

sometimes they don't die. And that's a good thing, but, when they're caught in between, that's really difficult."

"Isn't that when you get called in?"

"Sometimes. Not everybody really understands what I do," she noted, "so it means sometimes I get called in when it's too late. I've even been called in for bodies already cooling."

At that, Mariana gasped in shock.

Cara nodded. "And what am I supposed to tell them? I can't bring people back from the dead. Well, I mean, not unless they're still connected and ready to come back," she added. "Most of the time, people have absolutely no wish to come back," she murmured. "No matter how much they were loved here."

"That's got to be hard," Mariana murmured.

"Very. Well, for me, I mean. It's a decision the patient has already made. It's got nothing to do with me really, except that I get to be the bearer of the bad news." She frowned.

"That sucks."

"Yeah, it does, and the living rarely take it well. Most of the time, they don't take it well at all," she explained. "They think I'm either lying or making it up, not willing to help, wanting money or something. It's"—she raised both hands, palms up—"what I can say? It's sad. It's also painful."

And, with that, Cara walked over to the kitchenette, poured a cup of coffee, and returned her attention to her laptop. She was thankful when the women went back to work. Cara ignored everything else going on around her. It was hard though; it took a considerable amount of will to go through her emails, although there was one light at the end of the tunnel. She was being contacted about another case.

She immediately sent out a message, asking for more details. As soon as she got them, she'd have to sit down somewhere quiet and go in on an energy level to see if she could actually do anything in this particular case.

Lots of times she could do nothing, but, if there was a chance she could help, she would do what she could. That also would mean getting out of here, and she brightened at that idea. It was good timing.

When there was excited talk in front of her, she pulled off her headset, looked over at the women, and realized Mariana had left with her son. Lorelei wasn't around now, but Tasha and Sophia were talking excitedly.

Cara got up, hating that her curiosity overrode her emotions, but she could also feel that clenching of her heart to think that Rick was in the midst of something, without her support. She walked over, then asked, "What's going on?"

"They're in the house," Tasha said, "and you were right. Two bodies."

Cara nodded, still wondering what the excitement was about. "And?"

"And one live body."

She stared at her. "Really? Did they just arrive?"

"We're not sure," Tasha replied. "I just got a text."

Cara stared at the screen in front of her, but there was an odd abnormality in front. "All I can tell you is that whole scenario looks wrong to me, though this isn't the type of work I do."

"I get that." Tasha nodded and also studied the images.

Cara couldn't really explain what she saw. "I'm not used to seeing anything like this," she murmured, then shrugged. "But I have to trust that you guys know what you're doing." She turned around slowly, deliberately forcing herself to walk away.

"Unless you can sense anything wrong in any of the team's health." Sophia suddenly looked at her. "We don't have anything else to go by on that."

"Sure you do." Cara faced her. "You all have connections with the various men, don't you?"

They looked at each other and nodded slowly.

"But they're new connections," Tasha stated. "Except for Mariana, we don't really have anything other than like a Spidey sense as to where they are when they're doing something. We're learning to communicate telepathically, but we're not there yet."

"*New* connections?" Cara murmured, looking at the women. "As in, *love* connections?"

"Is that what you call it?" Sophia asked the other woman.

Tasha shrugged. "Damon and I had a connection before, but we didn't act on our personal feelings because it was complicated. We worked together," she explained. "We both were so busy trying to deny what was happening that we were awkward around each other. He didn't want to have our jobs be complicated or my safety compromised, and I just stuck around to do the job so I could stay close to him. Yet our conversations were stilted and uncomfortable. But, come to find out, everybody else knew we were a great match."

"Men are funny," Cara said, thinking about it. "All that really did—adding in the love aspect to an existing relationship—was to reinforce the connection because energy is energy, whether it's positive or negative."

"I hadn't considered that." Tasha frowned. "So you're saying that, because we were in close proximity, that energy between us grew and developed, even if we didn't really acknowledge it?"

"Absolutely. It's up to you guys what you do with it though."

"Yeah, well, Damon's not arguing about it now," Tasha said smugly.

"Of course not," Cara added. "Once the attack on the whole group happened, everybody had to reevaluate their lives and the people in them."

"So do you think that is also what Rick is doing right now?" Sophia asked.

"No, Rick is just being an idiot," Cara replied clearly.

At that, the other women gasped and then burst into laughter.

"He's male," Sophia agreed. "I think he's allowed his quota of being stupid."

Cara shrugged. "As long as he doesn't *do* anything stupid." She smiled and relaxed a bit, enjoying the company. "I might have another job lined up," she shared, "which would actually be perfect for me right now."

"In what way?" Tasha asked, looking at her with concern.

"It would help me to disconnect from this one." And, with that, she sat down back at her laptop.

RICK STARED DOWN at the two bodies, both with a single bullet to the back of the head.

"Execution style," Terk noted grimly.

"Yes." Then Rick motioned to the man they'd tied up and brought inside with them, one who was captured sneaking around outside. "Do you think he's got anything to do with it? Or is he just a nosy neighbor?" Rick glared at the man, who even now was quivering in his boots as he stared back at him.

"I didn't have anything to do with this," the frightened man cried out.

"Are you sure?" Rick asked in disgust. "You were caught skulking around outside, and, in here, we find two dead bodies."

"But I didn't kill them." he cried out. "I promise."

"So, this is what you mean by cleaning up?" Rick murmured to Terk.

Terk nodded. "Everywhere we go. It's like they're two steps in front of us."

"Have you considered tracking?"

"Meaning?" He stopped, facing Rick.

"Is there any chance, while we were down and out, that somebody put a tracking mechanism in our heads or something?"

Terk sucked in his breath.

Damon, who was beside Terk, shook his head. "I don't think any of us considered that," he noted cautiously. "Although we did pull some simple low-range device from Mariana's neck. What brought that thought to you?"

"Cara," Rick replied succinctly.

Terk studied him. "I can see how she has made you question all kinds of things," Terk noted, "but I can't imagine that very many people are out there can do what she does."

"Maybe not, but it's obvious that she could track me and probably still can." He turned, looking around, frowning.

"And, of course, we've met a lot of people who didn't

have the scrupulous standards she has," Damon noted in a conciliatory tone.

"At least we hope so," Rick muttered.

"Are you really angry at her?" Damon asked. "Or is this just an emotional reaction?"

"I don't know what I am," Rick snapped. "It feels like something's there that wasn't there before, and I don't know how to explain it."

Terk looked at him steadily. "And again I think you need to take a look at that, when you have more time."

"More time? When will that be?" he murmured. "Seems like we're always caught up in the middle of something."

"We are at the moment, but that won't last forever."

"Maybe not," Rick agreed, "but I don't know how much longer I can go without knowing what the hell this all is."

At that, Terk nodded. "In that case, when we get back, you need sort it all out because that distrust will eat away at your own system."

He sighed. "Am I wrong to distrust it?"

"I don't know. Are you?" he asked. "I told you that I've vetted her. So now we have a different trust issue."

At that, Rick stilled. "No, you're right. I'm being an idiot."

"Doesn't matter whether you are or you're not," Terk noted. "You still need to sort it out because, if you don't trust her, and you don't trust me, then I'm not sure who does have your trust. You know that this team has to be 100 percent on board with everything that happens. Otherwise nobody is on board. If we can't trust each other, we can't succeed, and the stakes are too high right now to take any chances."

With that, Rick realized what he had done by bringing it

up. "I do trust you, Terk, completely," he stated strongly. "I've just never had the sensation of anybody else in my head like this."

"That's not true either," Damon argued. "You're the one who sends out the grounding energy all the time. We're all used to having you boost who we are. Maybe it's just the fact that this is somebody you didn't necessarily choose to let in yourself."

He stared at him in shock. "I never thought of it that way. Maybe there's something to that."

"You have to sort it out, man," Damon repeated. "You're the only one who can deal with it."

Rick nodded. "I hadn't …" He stopped and shrugged. "I hadn't considered that Cara could be sending her energy to me."

"Well, you probably should, before she's gone," Damon suggested.

"It's not like she can go anywhere," Rick stated dismissively. "I just need some time in my own head, yet without that pressure of knowing she's there and looking at me all the time."

At first the men didn't say anything to that.

But Damon added, "I don't know. All of what she can do, like the tracking concern, has merit because obviously somebody seems to get to wherever we'll be ahead of us. And that's a security concern, regardless of who and how they're doing it. It would be much better if we could figure out how the bad guys are doing that, so we could track it back to them."

Just then their phones buzzed. Rick pulled his out first. "Tasha says there's a drone."

Immediately Terk lifted his phone and called her.

"You're on Speakerphone. Where is the drone?"

"Sophia picked up a drone outside the house," Tasha stated. "I don't know to what extent these things can fly or can go to various places, but, if you step out of that house, I think you'll be in danger."

"Thanks for the heads-up." Terk put away his phone. "Somebody tracked us here."

"Not necessarily," Damon argued. "I mean, it could be that they're just here to clean up their mess. Maybe they even saw this idiot skulking around outside."

"Hey," their captive interrupted. "All kinds of weird shit happens around here. Pardon me for being curious. And you guys haven't explained what you're doing here either." At that, Terk gave him his most ominous flat stare, and the man immediately shut up. "I won't tell anybody you were here," their prisoner stated honestly.

Terk shook his head. "Nope, you won't."

And that was enough to make the other guy moisten his lips and start to panic. "I promise I won't, really."

"Everybody says that," Terk said carelessly. "Doesn't help us at all right now. You're the one who has probably brought them all in and caused this dustup."

"Me? Why?"

"You were likely seen poking around," he explained. "And these guys couldn't take a chance, so they came in and shot their own guys to get rid of witnesses."

"But nobody else was here," their captive wailed.

"Did they go outside?"

"Yeah, they did," he said, "but they didn't shoot them out there." He stared at Terk and Rick.

Rick shook his head. "I wonder if they did though."

"What do you mean?" Terk asked.

"Well, what if they shot them with something, and, when they came back inside, it took them a little while to die."

"Yeah, but they got bullets in the back of their heads."

"Sure," Rick agreed, "but is that what killed them?"

Terk nodded. "I see what you're saying. You think they might have done something to incapacitate them slowly."

"What if they were dosed with some chemical, and they raced inside, but it was already too late?"

"So, like the drone could have sprayed them. They would have run inside. Then somebody comes along later and made sure they were done for."

Their prisoner agreed. "That's not a bad explanation."

Damon looked over at the guy. "What did you actually see?"

"Not much," he replied reluctantly. "Honestly my wife urged me to check it out in the first place." They looked at him, and he shrugged. "There's been enough strange goings-on that she's been getting worried."

"With good reason, apparently." Damon looked around.

"What the hell does this mean?"

"It means that your life is in danger," Terk stated. "Everybody who has seen these guys has been taken down, even the ones who work for them. So, regardless of your involvement," he added, "it's about to come to a full stop."

"I didn't have anything to do with them," he wailed in a panic. "What do you mean they're taking them out?"

Terk motioned at the two dead men on the ground. "Just like this. We don't know who is running this operation, but they are taken down every person involved." Just then his phone buzzed again. He looked at it. "Merk is outside."

"Good, are we leaving it to him?"

"Yeah, we are," Terk stated. "I'll be paying him off for a lifetime after this."

"What about this guy?" Rick asked, pointing to the snoopy neighbor.

"I don't know what to say. We'll wait for Merk and see what he suggests."

At that, the door back door opened, and Merk walked inside, his face grim. "Yeah, I saw the drones, though I'm not sure what's going on with them. They're a little high, almost like they're doing reconnaissance."

"We were wondering." Terk pointed at the two bodies. "Apparently the dead guys were outside earlier. We were wondering if maybe the drone shot them with some poison or something, trying to get them back inside and fall down here. Then somebody came and finished the job with a bullet."

Merk walked around, took a look at the bodies, and whistled. "Wow. They are not missing much when it comes to cleaning up, are they? Although they could have shot them outside with the drones."

"But we wouldn't have come inside, if we found these bodies outside." Terk added quietly, "And that's definitely been an ongoing concern."

Merk nodded. "I came in through the garage, so I didn't have to deal with the drones."

"Good thinking." Terk nodded. "That will give us a little bit more exit room. One issue we have now is what to do with this guy." He pointed at their live prisoner.

"Who is he?" Merk looked over at him, walking closer to stand above him. "What the hell is your involvement in this mess?"

"Nothing, nothing at all," he squeaked out. "Honest. I'm just a neighbor."

He snorted. "You believe that?" he asked Terk.

Terk shrugged. "We've come up against nosy neighbors many times before. They just don't get any smarter."

"Nosy neighbor, huh? Jesus." Merk shook his head. "You know that there's a reason why these guys like to move in the dark and not have anybody around them," he murmured, "and that's so they don't get seen. The minute people start poking around, the bad guys get antsy and they start killing."

Their prisoner's eyes got wider and wider, and the team talked like the neighbor wasn't even here.

"So, what do we do with him?" Terk murmured. "I hate to see him get shot, if he's not involved."

"He's already involved," Merk stated. "You know that. You can see it yourself."

"I know," he agreed. "It's a pisser though. I really didn't want to have to deal with any other bodies today."

Merk stared at him. "Since when do you deal with them?"

Terk grinned. "I did tell you that I love you, right, brother?"

He snorted. "I'm just trying to keep you alive and to get through this nightmare you've got yourself into."

"The fact that every time I turn around, there are more bodies is just making my life hell too. Who will you call for this time?"

"MI6. Who else?" He grinned. "And believe me. They're not happy."

At that, Terk smiled. "Say hi to Jonas for me."

Merk snorted. "Yeah, if I do that, he'll probably come

after you. He keeps asking me if you're involved."

"And what do you tell him?"

"I don't tell him anything," Merk stated. "There has been a lot of talk about some attack on your unit."

"I'm sure the government had to do something to cover it up."

"Well, what they're saying versus what actually happened is a different story," Merk noted.

"And how that narrative is working through the system is something we have to keep an eye on," Terk noted.

Rick agreed. "Well, if you can handle this and him," he said, with a pointed look at their guest, "that would be very helpful."

"And you, what will you do?" Merk asked.

"We'll tear apart the house," Rick replied, with a smile.

"I'll be here for that, so we'll just leave this guy where he is for the moment, and I'll contact Jonas to see what he wants to do with him."

"MI6 might be very interested in him," Terk said. "If nothing else, they should do a full check on his taxes."

At that, the man started to yell, "Just let me go. Let me go. I didn't do anything."

"No, but remember that whole thing about nosy neighbors?" Terk asked him. "Yeah, that's what got you where you're at right now."

And the guy got quiet, but tears were in his eyes.

Rick nodded. "Pretty amazing how much people come to a complete understanding of their actions as soon as you mention taxes."

Damon shrugged, then looked over at Merk. "I think he's probably okay to let go. I just don't know that he won't get killed when he steps outside."

"He probably will," Terk said.

At that, the guy frowned. "I heard that. If I'm in danger, what about my wife?"

"I don't know. Where is she?"

"I left her outside," he stated in panic. "She was waiting for me."

"So, does that mean she's about to come inside the door?" he asked, looking at him in surprise.

"I don't know."

At that, Terk got an odd look on his face. He turned to Merk and reached out a hand.

Merk looked at his brother. "God damn it."

Terk nodded slowly. He cast a glance back at the neighbor. "I think it's already too late."

CHAPTER 8

CARA GOT A response to her email faster than she expected and quickly read the description of the case. It was a fourteen-year-old boy who had been in a car accident. He was in a coma, and the family was desperate to try anything that could bring him back out. He'd already been comatose for three weeks and showed no signs of coming back to full awareness. She frowned at that.

She immediately sent a response, asking for the medical records, stating that she refused to look at any case without that type of background information and that she only took on cases where she felt she could do something. In this case, she wasn't exactly sure anybody could do anything, but it was too early to tell. Then went back and started thinking about her own apartment, trying to figure out what she wanted to do.

Even before this assignment had come up with Terk, she had been wondering about letting her apartment go and just renting short-term or maybe even hoteling it for a while. Traveling sounded pretty decent too, given the circumstances she was currently under, but it was all in theoretical states at present. Nothing she could really do right now until she was fully disconnected from Rick and this case.

She was working on it, but, every time she went to yank out more of her energy, she found resistance. She wasn't sure what the resistance was, but it caused her some trouble. Again it was different because, often at this stage, they were either awake and had other people to love them, so she could hand them off, or they'd crossed over to the other side, and she would be separated from her patient that way. It was all a bit of a mess with Rick, and she didn't quite know how to handle it, but she was working on it.

Nothing quite like knowing you had some shit to deal with to help you get your act together but not being in a position to deal with it. Finally sensing a restlessness that she didn't know how to address, she got up and wandered toward the commercial kitchen, finding Mariana putting together a meal. "So, do you know something I don't know?" she asked, with a note of humor.

Mariana looked at her, smiled. "I can't imagine what that would be. I just know that people need to be fed, and it gives me something to do on a regular basis, a way to contribute."

"I get that, and, in fact, I'm almost jealous," Cara admitted. "I was fully occupied before, caring for Rick, and now I'm at loose ends."

"And was there actually stuff to do?" she asked. "I'm not trying to question what you do at all, but, I mean, it seems like it's all in the mind."

"Lots of it is," she confirmed, "but a lot of it isn't. A lot of energy work entails keeping Rick connected yet isolated, without other people interfering. In his case, it was mostly the rest of his team. I got to know their energy pretty well because of that constant clearing out of those connections. I was always blocking their energies as they reached out, particularly Brody."

"Wait." Mariana frowned. "I haven't met Brody." Mariana stared at Cara. "Nobody here is named Brody."

Cara frowned at that. "*Huh*, I'll have to talk to Terk about it then."

"Well, for all you know," she said, "that could be one of the bad guys."

At that, the two women stared at each other. Cara shrugged. "I don't know what to say to that. Again I'll have to wait for Terk."

They nodded.

Cara looked at Mariana and the mess around her. "I don't suppose I could do anything to help you here?" She looked at Mariana expectantly. "I'm desperate for something to take my mind off things. I'm waiting for some medical records to come in on another potential case, which will keep me occupied, but right now I'm at loose ends and struggling."

"Well now, there'll always be potatoes to peel in my world," Mariana said, motioning at the large bag in front of her.

"You don't just do countrified with the skins on?"

"Depends on what I'm making." Mariana laughed. "But, if you have a need to keep your hands busy," she noted, "the potatoes await."

"Got it." Cara immediately picked up a small paring knife and got to work on them.

Only a few minutes later, Mariana looked over at her. "You're serious, aren't you?"

"Serious about what?"

"Well, for one thing, you needed something to work on. And, two, you're heading off on another job."

"I can't stay here," she explained, "and that's what I do."

Mariana nodded slowly. "Somehow I don't think it'll be

that easy."

"Why not?" Cara asked in astonishment. "This is an awkward stage. I get that, but Rick won't want me to stick around."

"I wouldn't be so sure of that," Mariana stated, "and it sure doesn't take any energy worker to understand that."

"What? What do you mean?" Cara asked, looking at her, puzzled.

"It doesn't take a magician to see that something is between you two."

"Yes, but that's just because of the healing energy work," Cara said dismissively. "Besides, he has made it pretty clear that he's upset with me over it all."

"He can be as upset as he wants," she replied, "but that doesn't change the fact that you did what you needed to do to keep him alive. Whether he likes it or not, that's on him, not you."

Just then, the connecting door opened, and, sure enough, in walked Rick. He stared at Cara. "Did I just hear part of a conversation that included my name?"

"Maybe."

Terk came in beside him, took one look at the coffeepot and his face lit up.

"You guys drink way too much coffee," Cara quipped, as she held a cup herself, so she was hardly one to talk.

As soon as Terk had a cup in his hand, Mariana said, "Look. I know that this has nothing to do with me, but Cara just made a statement about something that has us both confused." At that, Terk turned toward Cara, waiting on her to tell him more.

Cara shrugged. "I said that part of the final elements of my job that I was doing for your friend here"—she made a dismissive wave of her hand in Rick's direction—"was clearing away the healing energy."

Terk immediately nodded. "Yeah, that's a pretty common thing." He looked over at Mariana. "What part was confusing?"

Mariana continued. "Cara said she had figured out the energy coming to Rick came from the team, particularly from someone named Brody."

Terk's eyebrow shot up. "Brody?" he asked in astonishment.

Mariana nodded. "Then we realized that neither of us knew who that was."

Rick stepped forward. "Jesus Christ. Are you serious?"

"Yes, but you're not telling me who he is," Cara replied.

"Brody's one of the team," Terk agreed quietly. "One that we haven't had a whole lot of success in communicating with. At least I haven't."

"Have you still got that heavy shield up?" Cara asked Terk.

"Of course," he confirmed.

"Well, maybe you need to lighten it because Brody is out there, and he's been reaching out. I just didn't know who he was."

"I wish you'd told me earlier," Rick noted, fascinated.

"Tell you what?" she asked. "I was working, and it wasn't for me to dissect everybody in your world. My job was to try to keep you alive."

"I CAN'T BELIEVE that you were picking up Brody," Rick stated.

She looked at him directly for the first time since he had walked in. He almost felt like it was a benediction, as if it was a final acceptance in some way, except he wasn't expecting that reserved look in her gaze. He frowned at that.

"Is he a special friend of yours?" she murmured.

Rick nodded. "Absolutely. To all of us, but Brody and I were probably the closest. Brody had a special ability," Rick explained. "He made us all feel like we were his best friend."

Cara smiled. "That's because, to you guys, I'm sure he is. The fact of the matter is, he's out there, searching. He's lost, and I guess I didn't help him." She frowned, as she looked over at Terk. "Can you contact him?"

"I've been trying." He stared at her. "Which is why I'm so surprised that you picked him up."

"Well, he came knocking," she said. "What was I supposed to do? At any time I can have dozens of souls knocking."

"Let him in," Rick said. "Can you contact him now?"

"I don't know." She frowned. "I closed all the doors."

At that, everybody stopped and stared at her.

She shrugged. "That's what I needed to do." She didn't elaborate.

Then Rick realized that it was exactly what she needed to do, mostly because of him. He looked over at Terk. "I can handle this." He looked over at Cara. "Let's go talk."

She shrugged. "I don't have anything to say."

He frowned at her. "I do."

She glared at him. "That's nice, but I'm really not in the mood."

"Too damn bad," he stated forcibly. "We obviously have a few things to sort out here."

She gave him a stare that would set anybody's nerves on

edge.

"It would be nice if you would go talk with him," Tasha urged, as she joined in the conversation. "Brody is a very important part of this team. If he's lost, then …"

Rick heard the tears in her voice. He nodded. "And, in order for Cara to do that"—he faced her—"you have to open some doors."

"I have no intention of opening any doors," she stated firmly. "Some doors need to stay closed."

"Does the door to Brody need to stay closed?"

She frowned. "I don't know. Depends on what wavelength he's using."

The others just stared.

She shrugged. "I can't explain it. My methodology isn't exactly something that is taught."

"Maybe it should be," Terk noted in fascination.

"You're the one who contacted me." She shrugged. "So you obviously know more about me than I necessarily do."

He laughed. "No, I wouldn't say that at all, but I do find that every person I meet who has an ability in this field, all have some things that are self-taught, things that they've learned all on their own, that they find hard to describe."

"Well, I'm no different," she agreed. "It's not like I can turn around and say I do A, B, C, D and expect that it will work for you. It might. It might not."

"The bottom line," Wade added, stepping forward, "is regardless of whatever issues you have with Rick, can you contact Brody and let him know that we're here and give him a way to contact us?"

She frowned and looked at each and every one of them individually.

Rick could sense her hesitation. "Come on. Let's go

talk." She remained reluctant, but he managed to get her to agree.

"I better not miss dinner because of you," she snapped.

"You won't. I promise. I'll give you mine if that's the case."

She just glared at him, and he heard a silent collective sigh from those around him.

When he got her to her room, he closed the door behind him and leaned against it. "Look. I know that you're having some struggles with everything that's gone on and that I haven't helped. I'll be the first to admit that."

She didn't say anything. She just walked over to the bed and sat down.

He added, "I apologize for that. It was a bit of a shock—all of it's been a bit of a shock. … I've always been a loner, a little bit of a renegade, and I haven't necessarily handled some of this news very well."

She just gave him that same look again.

"You know that I'm really starting to dislike that look on your face right now."

She smirked. "Good. Now, if you'll just go away, I'll see if I can contact Brody."

He hesitated because ultimately that's what he really wanted. "Brody is a really good guy. If there's anything you can do to help him, please try."

"I can't do anything while you're interfering," she stated.

"Is there anything I can do?"

"Yes, leave me alone."

He groaned, stepped forward. "Look, Cara. I won't do that."

She frowned. "What are you talking about?"

"None of this makes any sense." He shook his head. But

he scooped her up, until she was standing again, then grabbed her on either side of her face and kissed her. Not a simple kiss, but something that caught him by an unseen force and took him into depths that he had no idea existed.

When he lifted his head, he saw a glazed look in her eyes. He nodded. "And that's how I feel too. I don't know what magic you're working here, my dear, but I am truly caught. And maybe that's part of the anger, the frustration, that I'm feeling. I don't know." He shook his head. "I've never felt anything like this before, and what really tears me apart the most is worrying that it's not real."

And, with that, he turned and walked out of her room.

CHAPTER 9

CARA SAGGED DOWN back onto the bed, not sure what had just happened, but, knowing from the energy surge between them, all of her attempts to break contact had failed. And now that it had been reinforced by his actions, she had no idea what to do about it. The only thing she could really do at the moment was try to collect her thoughts and focus on Brody.

The thought of somebody lost out in the ethers was heartbreaking, but she had no idea that's what had happened to him. Castigating herself for not having checked into it earlier, she dropped her head and opened herself back up again. She knew it would hurt.

She knew that the onslaught of souls seeking her help would be beyond painful, but she also knew that, in order to save Brody, she would have to do this. So, if she suffered a little, it would be minor compared to what he was currently enduring, though nobody ever cared about that part, and they shouldn't, she tried to tell herself firmly. It's enough to be of service to Brody. Even if Cara didn't always have a happy ending.

At the moment, based on what Rick had just done, she had no way of knowing if there would be a happy ending for her and Rick. All she could do was carry on as usual and wait for Rick to see what he wanted out of their connection.

As soon as she opened up the energy highway, she checked on all the threads that she had kept in the loop. There was one to Terk, which was just basically common sense, considering that they both had the ability to communicate that way. She kept that connection on Pause all the time, as did he. And then there was the one to Rick. She quickly dashed past that one, so she didn't have to deal with the heartache and the questions clamoring through her brain.

Instead she headed out onto the open road, looking to see who was crying out, who was calling out, and who was in need of help. She knew when she put out such a call that she would get inundated in ways that could be catastrophic, but, with everybody wanting her to do this, she felt bound and determined to follow through.

She sagged deeper and deeper, as she separated more from the physical plane, letting herself flow into the ethers freely. She sent out a strong message, directed completely toward Brody. As soon as she heard a half cry in the distance, she refocused and called out to him.

"Here. I'm here," Brody said.

And she realized, not only was he lost but he'd been lost for some time. As soon as he realized that she was here and that she was here to help, he latched on with a ferocity that she'd expected but, at the same time, was still almost impossible to deal with. Gasping for control, she tried hard to get him to calm down, so she could do what she needed to do. However, Brody reacted almost in a panic, worried that she would disappear. So Cara took over and was left with no option. She not only disconnected but she knocked out Brody at the same time. When she slowly came to, Terk was in her bedroom, staring at her, and he wasn't alone. Rick was at her side. They both had concerned expressions on their faces.

Rick immediately bent down. "I'm so sorry. We didn't think about the cost to you."

She didn't say anything. She blinked, trying to refocus on where she was.

Terk murmured, "And having paid that cost, did you find him?"

"He's there," she replied. "I had to knock him out."

Terk nodded in understanding, but Rick didn't seem to have the same ability to detach.

"May I ask why?" he asked, with great difficulty. "And when you said you knocked him out …"

"Hopefully his spirit is not running around going crazy at the moment," she explained slowly.

"I'll take that as a good thing," Rick noted quietly, "but why?"

But Terk answered for her. "Because he would have latched on to her like a drowning man," he replied, "particularly if he was panicked."

Rick looked over at her for confirmation, and she nodded.

"Yes, he was definitely frantic, and it was building. He's calm at the moment. I've connected, and I still have that connection."

Terk nodded and smiled. "And, for that, I thank you."

"It would have been good if you'd told me that he was out there like this," she directed to Terk.

He nodded. "It would have been. I see that now. It never occurred to me that you could connect with more than just Rick at the same time. You need to know other team members are still out there too."

She opened her eyes wide. "You're kidding."

"That's part of the reason why I needed help."

Terk had said it so simply that she knew it was true. "Right, you're connected to all of them. I don't know how you're even doing that and still standing, breathing."

"I was connected to Brody, but he got free somehow," Terk murmured. "And I don't really understand how that happened."

She stared at him for a long moment. "Well, that might explain the level of panic in his voice. He feels like he's completely lost out there."

"And he is, to a certain extent," Terk agreed.

"When he comes to again, I'll funnel that energy in gently," she explained, "and I'll let him know he's not alone."

"Thank you, Cara," Rick said gently.

She nodded. "Now, if you don't mind, I think I'll just rest a while." She looked around to find she was lying on the floor. "I gather I collapsed."

Rick shrugged. "I don't know. I just found you like this. I wanted to pick you up and put you on the bed, but Terk wouldn't let me."

"No. Don't. If you ever find me like this—in an altered state—*don't touch*," she ordered. "You'd pull me back, and sometimes you might pull something back with me."

He stared at her, his jaw wide open.

She smiled and nodded. "It's not all sunshine and roses in my work. I must have a lot of safeguards, and they're there for me and for my patient." On that note, she slowly rolled over, got up on her knees, and made her way to the bed. She waved them off. "I just need to collapse for a while now." And, with that, she sagged down onto the bed. She knew Rick wouldn't leave her quite so easily but she hoped he would. She looked over at Terk. "Take him out of here, will you?"

"No," Rick argued. "I'm staying."

She groaned. "What? To watch me while I sleep?"

"Why would something like that take so much energy out of you?"

She didn't answer, hoping that Terk would, and, when he did, it wasn't something that Rick was necessarily prepared to hear.

"She disconnected because of you," Terk explained. "So when she reconnected just for the purpose of reaching out to Brody, she had to open everything up again, so she wasn't ready for the energy onslaught, but it probably came with a lot more than she had been prepared for."

"You could say that." She started to drift off. She murmured, "They're hunting you."

Terk stepped forward and, in a low voice, asked, "Where are they?"

"Close, within miles."

"Can you track them?"

"Don't need to. They're tracking you. Open your senses," she murmured. She felt a lethargy that she hadn't expected taking over.

"Keep your senses open," Terk murmured, "for your own safety."

"I can't," she whispered, "too much pain."

"It will ease," he murmured.

"Not enough. Danger," she said. "All around you is danger."

At that, her eyes drifted closed.

"CAN WE BELIEVE everything she's getting?" Rick asked in a hushed voice.

"Yes," Terk said. "She's one of the most powerful energy workers I've ever met."

"Too bad you couldn't bring her on board," he said.

"Me too, but her forte has always been healing."

"Until now?"

"Not until now."

"What about Brody?" Rick asked. "Is it safe to leave him like that?"

"If she says he's connected, he'll wake up with a sense of being connected. He may not reach out to you or me, but, as long as she wakes up not too long from now, she'll let us know if he reaches back."

"God. I was completely wrong about her, wasn't I?" Rick asked.

"On many levels," Terk agreed, "but it's up to you to sort through all that."

"Thanks," he said. "A little bit of warning would have been nice."

"You weren't ready to hear it," Terk stated simply. "Just because something is happening doesn't mean people are ready to deal with it."

"Do you know what it is that's happening?"

"I can guess," he replied. "She couldn't have made the connection she made to you without having poured her heart and soul into it."

"And then, when she did, I stomped on it," Rick added in a low tone. "I feel awful about that."

"I know, but don't beat yourself up over it," Terk said, "and definitely don't take on something that you're not prepared to put your own heart and soul into as well because you'll break her. She had to give you her all to keep you alive, and, in order for that to happen, she had to open herself up to so much more than she normally would. It worked. She saved you. Maybe you're not ready for the bond that came with it," Terk added, "and don't even begin to make it sound like you are. It's not a *fake it till you make it* thing. She'll know your line, and she'll withdraw well and truly in advance."

"I have no idea what I'm feeling," he murmured. "It's too bizarre. But I can tell you that we're bonded in a way I've never felt before."

"It is bizarre, but you're also blessed," Terk noted, "because the connection you have right now is priceless."

"But is it really what it feels like?"

"Well, I don't know." Terk smiled. "What does it feel like?"

"I hate to say it because I've never felt it before, so maybe love?"

"At that point, it's love at a spirit level," Terk said. "It's up to you whether it becomes anything more than that."

"God," he said in a rush. "Just to even think that something like that is possible blows my mind."

"I know. Pretty heavy stuff, isn't it?"

"It's unbelievable," Rick said. "Seriously unbelievable. It's so addicting, and there's something else." He stared at Terk, wondering if he should even put this in words. "I'm not sure … that I could even let her go now. It's like … she's a part of me somehow."

"That's because you still don't understand. In order to keep you alive, she had to become a part of you. For better or for worse, you guys are connected on all levels now," he murmured, then turned to leave. "And remember. That was a price she was prepared to pay to save you, so consider that when she wakes up—and every other time you think about being less than nice to her."

And, with that, Terk walked out, leaving Rick alone to stare down at the sleeping woman who had saved his life, without regard to what it would cost her. He felt more like an ass than ever before.

CHAPTER 10

WHEN CARA WOKE up, she was groggy and, for whatever reason, sore. She got up slowly, taking her time, knowing that, having opened up the energy floodgates, even though she had tried hard to separate what she could and could not let through, it would have an effect on her. A hot shower usually helped, and, by the time she slowly made her way out to the big commercial kitchen, looking for the coffee she was in desperate need of, she was grateful to find the only person there was Mariana.

"Hey." Mariana looked at her critically. "You look like shit."

Cara gave her droll look. "Yeah, that's what happens when you go fishing out on the ethers."

At that, Mariana winced. "And we didn't help you on that at all, did we?"

"I get it. You all have a relationship with this person."

"Not me," she said, "but I do know now that he's very much a part of this team and nobody wants to consider that he's lost out there."

"Well, I can't say that he's still not lost at the moment either."

"Did you contact him?" she asked hesitantly.

"More or less, but that doesn't mean he's responding."

"Oh, shit," she replied. "I never even thought of that. I

guess it's not that simple, is that?"

"Nothing is that simple," Cara noted, "and unfortunately that just makes me feel worse."

"And that's not on you at all," Mariana stated immediately. "Come on. Sit down and get some coffee. You really do look like you need energy."

She nodded. "It's either that or go back to bed and see if I can sleep again, but I've been awake for a while, tossing and turning anyway." She looked around. "Where is everybody?"

"Sophia and Tasha are on the computers, doing whatever it is they do, searches on whatever happened yesterday or something. Lorelei is working on her computer in her room." Mariana raised both palms. "The men have gone back to the same house, looking for something in particular"—she shook her head—"and hopefully they're also picking up supplies because, since they were going out, I gave them a list." She smiled.

"Ah. Foodstuffs are an ongoing problem here, isn't it?"

"Well, problems are relative around here," she noted. "We're okay financially, as far as I understand. It's a matter of not attracting attention when we shop, so nobody really understands how many people I'm trying to feed here."

"I'm sorry that fell to you and that I've added to it," she murmured. "You really don't have to feed me."

"What will I do?" she asked, looking at her in surprise. "Hold your dinner and make you work for it or something?"

Cara laughed at that. "Well, you and I both know plenty of people out in the world would do just that."

"Unfortunately I do."

Cara looked around. "Where's your little guy?"

"He's in there with the girls on a computer," she said, with an eye roll. "Sophia got him started on a computer game the other day, but thankfully he has to navigate through some educational challenges to earn playing time. He already adores computers."

"Wow, he'll be incredibly capable of that by the time he hits his teens."

"Yeah, he'll be incredibly capable before he ever gets into preschool at this rate," she noted, with a half smile. "Everybody here seems to be quite willing to teach him, and he's like a sponge."

"Yeah, that goes with the age too, doesn't it?"

"Have you ever worked with really young kids?" Mariana asked.

"A couple times." Cara smiled. "Those are the most rewarding, at least when they've got a chance."

"I suppose they probably accept some of this stuff easier than adults."

"Sometimes." She nodded. "They're also closer to having one foot in the grave because they haven't actually left."

At that, Mariana stared, her eyes going wide. "Oh, good Lord. I'm sorry I asked."

"Yeah, nothing is ever quite so simple." Cara grabbed a coffee and sat down at the table and bowed her head over the cup, just letting the heat bathe her forehead. If nothing else, this should make her feel better. She wasn't so sure about after that. When somebody spoke to her, she lifted her head to find Mariana asking her about food.

"Do you have anything?" Cara frowned. "I know you said you were after supplies."

"Oh, sure, I've got a system going now, so we're shopping ahead a bit. We've got too many mouths to feed to risk running out. And there's always toast and eggs, sandwiches, and basics like that," she explained. "Does anything sound good?"

"Actually eggs and toast sounds good," Cara said. "Protein will probably help a lot right about now."

"Okay, let me get you some." Mariana quickly brought out a fry pan and tossed in a couple eggs. She looked over at Cara. "Do you want some sausage, bacon, or something like that too? When the men come back in, they're always pretty worn down."

"Yeah, we all can be," Cara noted. "It depends on what we've been doing and all." She yawned and then nodded. "But just eggs and toast will be fine. I don't want to put you to any more work than I already have. If you've got peanut butter or something along that line, that would work too."

"What's everybody's fascination with peanut butter?" Mariana shook her head.

"For some of us, it becomes an instant rescue food, like when you come out and your blood sugar has dropped because of exertion? Blood sugar doesn't affect energy, but energy definitely affects blood sugar."

Mariana blinked a couple times at that and then nodded. "That almost makes sense."

Cara laughed. "What you're doing is more valuable than what I'm doing," She reached for the plate with the eggs.

"Oh, don't say that," Mariana murmured. "Believe me. If you have any way to contact Brody, they will be all over you about it."

"Yeah, well, that's not necessarily so great," she admitted. "I'm already blaming myself for not having found out more when he first reached out to me. It's still so bizarre to think that he could even do it," she murmured.

"Anything these guys do is like that for me," Mariana murmured, "but I'm learning. It's slow going. I'm just taking in bits and pieces and trying not to get too overwhelmed."

"That's not a bad way to go," Cara agreed.

"It seems everything that goes on here is outside the norm, but they are sure good people. Yet Terk couldn't get you to join in, *hmm?*"

"At the time, I was helping a set of twins."

Mariana looked at her. "How old?" she asked hesitantly.

"They were four," she murmured.

"And did they live?" she asked, as if she couldn't help herself.

At that, Cara smiled and nodded. "In this case, they certainly did."

"Well, thank God for that." She stared at Cara in fascination. "That cannot be an easy job."

"No, and it's not only *not* easy, it can be heart-wrenching. But, in that case, they lived, and the parents welcomed them back into this reality with open arms. They're doing fine now."

"Even just your wording," she murmured.

She shrugged. "I don't even know what to say about it anymore. The people I work with have to be vetted very carefully. It's not the kind of work that I am comfortable sharing with a ton of people. I work with a few doctors, a few specialists, and people like Terk. Other than that, I don't tell anybody what I do. So, being here, it's both odd and refreshing. These abilities are accepted, and yet, at the same time, nobody really does what I do. So they don't really understand how or what's required."

"No, and I think some of them were wondering about that last night," Mariana stated. "You know, when you think about it, a lot was asked of you."

"I don't mind that. I want to help if I can. The problem

comes in when I can't actually do what they want."

"But you did contact Brody last night?" she asked hesitantly.

"Well, more like I put out breadcrumbs for him to follow, if he gets a chance to contact me again."

"That's something then," Mariana noted, "and nobody can blame you. You tried. It's just what it is."

"They will blame me," she said quietly, "because I did know he was there, and I didn't do anything about it."

"And why didn't you?"

She hesitated and then said, "Partly because I had no idea if he was a friend or an enemy. But mostly because I had my hands full just trying to save Rick."

"You didn't tell them that."

"They weren't ready to hear that," she replied, "especially not Rick."

RICK HAD BEEN standing in the doorway, leaning against the doorjamb, watching, regretting how tired Cara appeared to be. Hearing the words dropping freely from her mouth to Mariana made him realize what they'd asked of her, but the last comment she had made really hit home. He stepped forward, making it look as if he'd just come in, but she stiffened, and he realized that, only because she was so tired, she hadn't known he was here earlier.

She didn't even turn around when she asked, "Do you always listen in on conversations?"

"I wasn't trying to," he said, "but you're right. I should have let you know I was here."

She shrugged. "Maybe I did know."

"No, I suspect you wouldn't have shared anything if you had," he noted.

She continued to eat without saying anything more. He walked closer, grabbed a coffee, and then sat down beside her, noting that at least she was eating freely and well.

"I don't know how many times I'm supposed to say I'm sorry," he said, "but it's definitely going to need at least a few more times."

She stared at him, but again she didn't say anything.

It was that reserved demeanor that got him. It was like she'd spent so much of her life alone and not expecting anything good out of people that, whenever he said something, it seemed to be a complete surprise to her. "I get that you've spent a lot of time alone, but you don't have to stay that way."

She shrugged. "It's probably best."

"I don't think so."

"But then you don't know anything," she stated quickly.

He wanted to get angry, and certainly a part of him felt this guilt and an overwhelming need to find a way to break through her reserve, but he also knew that to use any pressure would just make things way worse. "Did you manage to get ahold of him?"

"Not necessarily," she replied, her answer almost even more frustrating. "I left the door open and a series of breadcrumbs for him to follow, if he can."

He let his breath out slowly. "And I guess that's the best that we can expect now."

"I can't bring him back from wherever he was," she explained. "When my energy replenishes, I will go see if there's been any movement."

"Movement?" he asked.

"On the pathway I left open," she said.

He nodded. "We'd appreciate you doing that." He hated that he acted so formal, but it seemed like the only way to really make this happen. He looked over to see Mariana frowning at him. He raised both hands in frustration. "And now you're looking at me like I'm doing everything wrong."

"No," she said, "but she needs love and understanding right now, not more work."

"I get that, but I'm afraid there's a limited amount of time."

"That's because you're coming from fear," Cara replied. "Brody's alive, and he's well enough to struggle, trying to fight his way back. I can tell that much."

"Well, that's something." Rick really wanted to ask more, but he hesitated. Then, realizing that he really needed to just give her a chance to eat and to relax, he asked, "Did you manage to get any sleep?"

"Not much, but that's just the way it works sometimes."

He frowned at that. "Do you ever run out of energy doing what you're doing?"

She shrugged. "There are ways to regenerate energy, so it depends."

He wasn't sure what to make of that answer, but he felt he could probe only so much. It was a relief when he heard someone coming, and Terk, Damon, Gage, and Wade walked in, each of them carrying boxes. When they saw Cara, an immediate welcome was on all their faces.

"Glad to see you're up." Terk smiled. "How's the head?"

She gave him a droll look. "Still attached."

He stared at her, startled for a moment, and then he laughed. "Man. I keep forgetting about that sense of humor of yours."

Rick wasn't sure he had even heard it. Her response to Terk had been off the cuff and instantaneous. Realizing that she had that sense of humor, and he just hadn't been privy to it was telling, because why would he be? He'd been more of an aggressor and an enemy in her world than a friend. Again he felt the same regrets eating at him. She wasn't being very forthcoming or giving him much in the way of options though.

Damon looked at her and hesitated. She didn't say anything. Then he frowned and spoke up. "It would be nice if you would volunteer information, so I don't have to ask, because asking makes it feel like I'm opening myself up to bad news."

"He's alive. He's well enough to struggle. I left a path, … a series of breadcrumbs."

Rick's, Damon's, and Wade's expressions all looked equally confused, but, when they caught sight of Terk, they seemed to be less so.

"That's probably the best thing you could do under the circumstances," Terk stated, with a nod.

"Somebody needs to explain that to me," Damon stated, a little more forceful than necessary.

Terk added, "She has given him a pathway. If he gets a chance to come out again, he should have no trouble finding it."

None of them appeared to be too certain of exactly what that meant, but, if Terk thought it was a good thing, they were all prepared to go with it. Obviously Damon wanted to ask more questions, but Terk waved him off.

Cara finished eating calmly, and afterward she got up and looked over at Terk. "I'll let you know." Then she turned and left.

Immediately the men turned to Terk. "She'll let you know what?"

"I presume," he said carefully, "that she's gone to take a look to see if Brody found the breadcrumbs."

At that, they all just froze. "And if he has?"

"Then she may bring him in," he noted, "but there is no guarantee that he's found them yet."

"Brody is strong," they all protested.

"I know, but that has nothing to do with it." Terk smiled at his team.

Damon nodded. "I know. I'm just frustrated."

"We're all frustrated, but you need to give Cara a little bit of space. What she's doing is not easy, and she's feeling horribly guilt ridden for not knowing Brody's connection to our team, up until now."

"Well, it does seem odd that she would have turned away somebody coming to her," Wade noted. "I really don't know who she is as a person, but that just seems like an odd thing to do."

"That's because you don't realize how connected she is to me—or was, I guess," Rick shared. "She didn't mention that information, except to Mariana. I just overheard her saying something about she was still heavily connected to me, so she took note of who it was but didn't dare attempt to let him in for fear of losing her hold on me or allowing the enemy in."

The men all pondered that for a moment.

"Does that mean she can only help one at a time?" Wade asked.

At that, Terk snorted. "How many can you help at that level at any time?" he asked. "She did a lot for Brody, in the sense that she tracked where he is and that she even got a name from him. Remember. Brody represents just one energy thread. Among so many more. We, as a team, are tied to one another. Closely. And we know how cluttered our minds can get with just a handful of us clamoring for attention. Consider how many more people could be talking to Cara, especially when you realize thousands upon thousands are trying to garner her attention, her help as a healer. Among all those souls calling out to her, she isolated this one tiny strand of energy, floating out in the ethers, because he represented a possible threat to Rick's healing. The fact that she could even put a name to Brody's energy was amazing."

They all immediately nodded. "I guess we're being a little harsh on her because we so desperately want to know that Brody is okay."

"She says that he is okay," Terk noted, "and I can also confirm that he's alive."

"That's huge," Wade said, and they all relaxed slightly.

"It is, but again we have to give her a little bit of time and also give Brody some time."

"I can't imagine floating for as long as that," Rick muttered.

"I know, and he's not the only one of us still out there," Terk reminded them.

"Are you thinking of asking her to help with Scott too?" Damon asked.

"Well, if you're going to," Tasha said from the doorway, "you might want to do it soon because she mentioned something yesterday about having been contacted regarding another client."

At that, Terk turned and stared at Tasha. "Seriously?"

She nodded. "And I didn't pry. I was determined to try and make her feel better."

"I know. I didn't say anything either." Sophia came in behind Tasha. "We just let her do her thing and gave her back her laptop. She seemed to enjoy hanging out with us, while she checked her email."

"Then she left again, and we assumed it all was happening in her own personal world."

"Which would have been what?" Terk asked.

"How do people normally contact her?" Sophia asked.

"I don't know," Terk admitted. "I had a number for her, and I checked out her energy first, to see just what stage of life she was at, before I reached out."

At that, they turned and stared. He shrugged. "When she works with clients like that, it can involve anything."

"Right," Wade murmured. "Hard to imagine the work she's been doing."

"And freely," Terk reminded them. "It takes an awful lot out of her—physically, emotionally, at a soul-deep level. She learns a lot, but she also gives a lot."

And, once again, Rick felt like he'd been given a slam to his heart. He looked back down the hallway where she had disappeared. "I wonder if I should go check on her."

"I'd wait a bit," Terk suggested immediately. "If she's gone looking for Brody, let's not split her focus."

Rick nodded. "Good point, but I just feel like we're running at cross-purposes."

"You are, with Cara," Terk confirmed, "and, yes, you have to resolve that personal issue, but we as a team also have to be careful to do it in such a way that it doesn't interfere with somebody else's ability to return."

But just then, Cara walked back in again, her face calm and composed. She looked over at Terk. "He found my breadcrumbs, but he's bouncing off someone else's energy. A

Scott. … If he's one of yours, he's in a similar boat to Brody."

Everybody froze, and then smiles burst forth. Terk's grin split his face wide. "Now that's excellent good news. Scott *is* one of ours. How did they both look?"

"Brody is still a bit lost, shaken, and confused. Scott is in a maze and hurting. Not on a physical level."

At the term, Rick turned to her. "Is there anything you can do for him?" he asked, looking worried. "For both of them?"

She studied him for a long moment. "I'm not sure that is part of what I should be doing." She turned to look at Terk.

"In what way?" he asked her.

"Scott's calling out for a woman."

The others all froze.

"A woman?" Rick asked.

"Yes, a woman. Somebody he knew. Somebody he cares about. He's searching for her in the ethers. Before I contact him, you need to tell me more about her."

"Who is she?" the team asked, looking at each other, clearly bewildered.

But Tasha stepped up. "Is he asking about Naira?" Tasha nodded, as she turned to look at Cara.

"What's the story, Tasha?" Cara asked.

"At one time, she was the love of Scott's life. But she ended up married to somebody else, and he headed off into the world as we know it," Tasha replied. "But he has never forgotten her."

"*Hmm,*" Cara murmured. "I definitely got a feeling of that energy being there."

"They were very close," Tasha added. "Her family caused some trouble between them, and it was enough that they split up over it. Yet I have no doubt that feelings still exist between them."

"If she turned around and married somebody else, the feelings must not have been all that strong," Damon noted.

"But I know that Scott still cared about her, and it's possible that he's still looking for her," Tasha murmured.

Cara frowned. "I'll have to see where he's at, when I go back in."

"So, will he be there, just waiting or something?" Rick asked. "Can you help him to, I don't know, get back into his natural world somehow?"

"The problem is, there are penalties and prices for some of that." She studied Terk directly, not even bothering to look at Rick. "So Terk will have to make some decisions on that."

"Right." Terk nodded. "I will take a look."

"Do that," Cara replied, "and time is of the essence."

He winced. "I'll talk to you in a bit then." Terk put down his cup, got up, and walked out of the room.

The others stared at her, but she ignored them.

"I get that you have some abilities that most of us haven't even heard of," Rick admitted. "It would help us to understand if you would elaborate slightly. If you want to, that is."

She frowned at him. "I thought you guys were on board with everything Terk does."

"Nobody knows everything Terk does," Rick stated. "Not even close."

"Ah." She nodded. "That fits too."

"Fits what?"

"The energy around you all," she replied, speaking to the whole group. "You're all very connected, but you've all been connected while still trying to give each other space. So you haven't necessarily made all the connections between you, as other families would."

"Well, that's because we're not blood family," Rick noted, "but I certainly consider these men my brothers."

She nodded. "And that much is evident, but always other relationships are involved in groups like this."

"You said there were signs of energy. So is there any chance that Naira is looking out for Scott?"

"I think she probably is, yes," Cara replied. "Though that doesn't mean she's free to be at the level he wants her at."

"Ouch," Sophia murmured. "Makes you wonder about fate."

"Fate is not so much a real thing, as compared to the free will that we each enjoy," Cara murmured, as she studied each of them slowly, one at a time. "You make decisions that affect everything that happens, and you learn from it. If you're lucky, you get a chance—or even a second chance. Some people will always go through life, feeling like they're isolated and separate from the rest of the world." Her grin flashed.

"For example, even in astrology, they say that Aquarians often feel like they don't quite fit in and don't quite belong to the family they're born into. It doesn't mean that they aren't in the right place. It just means that they have more lessons to learn."

"Oh, wow," Lorelei said in fascination. "I've always had an interest in astrology, but it always seemed like so much gobbledygook."

"Or just straight lies," Wade added, studying Cara.

Just then Terk stepped back in again. "I've contacted Naira and told her what happened."

"*What* happened?" Rick asked him.

"About Scott getting hurt in the attack on our team. In each case, I've looked for somebody in your world to let them know about that and the state of the person attached to them. In Scott's case, I never thought of her." He looked over at Tasha, with a frown. "Guess I should have asked you earlier, about both Scott and Brody. But Brody doesn't have anyone in his world for me to call. It would help a lot though."

Tasha shrugged. "Yeah, but you guys like to do a whole lot of that Lone Ranger thing," she murmured. "Sounds like Brody does too. Independent, arrogant, likely a loner." She swung her arms wide around the room. "Look at the lot of us. Each of us had a potential or an existing relationship that was kept secret from the other members of this team. Probably based on that misguided protection angle. But now we should all know better, right?" Again Tasha looked at every person in the room.

Terk nodded. "That's something else we should all be working on. If Scott and Brody can return to the land of the living, we get a chance at changing it."

"Good," Cara agreed. "We can do a lot to help, even if it's just by sharing information better."

"I get it," Terk noted quietly.

"What was Naira's reaction?" Rick asked. "Is she willing to help?"

"Shocked. Stunned really. I did ask what her personal circumstances were, and, though I'm certain she thought the questions were very odd, she did answer them. So I found out that she is currently divorced and free. She asked if she could come over and physically see Scott. She's arranging her flight."

"Well, that's something at least. It would be great if Brody had something to wake up to that would put a smile on his face," Mariana suggested. "I presume that's very important to their healing, to getting them back on this plane."

Everybody nodded.

"But that"—Terk turned to look at Cara—"brings up another question. What's this I hear about you being offered another job?"

She stiffened and looked at him. "Is that a problem?"

"Not necessarily. I get that this is what you do and that you're probably looking to settle the next step in your life, but frankly I'm a little concerned—security-wise—about how they contacted you."

Rick stared at her. Somehow he hadn't thought of her leaving. Yet … obviously it was her calling, her work, and he didn't want her to stay here just because of him. … Or did he?

"The same way everybody contacts me. By email. By phone sometimes." Cara studied Terk closely. "What's the problem?"

"I'm worried that it could be somebody involved with what we're dealing with here."

"So," she began, as she thought about it for a moment, "you're thinking that it's somebody trying to get to me?"

"I'm wondering about it," Terk agreed. "Would you allow us to take a look at whoever contacted you?"

She stared at him for a long moment. "I asked for the medical records on the patient, and I haven't heard back yet."

He nodded. "That would be your next logical step, wouldn't it?"

"Just part of it," she replied. "As always, a lot is going on all at once, and I have a lot to deal with."

"Of course," he murmured, "and you also have to make an assessment as to whether this new case is worth it or not."

"It's more an assessment as to whether or not I can help." Cara shrugged. "Not everybody wants to hand over medical records, but, if they're serious about getting my help, it's something I have to see."

Terk motioned to her. "Can you get your laptop, please?"

Something about his tone of voice made it clear that declining wasn't an option. She groaned. "If your BS is infiltrating my work life …"

"You knew it was a possibility," he noted gently.

"Possibilities, probabilities, and likelihoods are all vague terms," she argued. "This could be something very concrete."

"This could lead us to whoever is after you, and, if that's the case, we need to figure out who it is and capture them. Afterward, maybe we can get your life freed up, and you can go on to do whatever you choose to do next." Terk waved toward the connecting door. "I suggest we all move to the computer room."

Cara nodded and slipped from the big kitchen, with the rest of them following her.

Terk turned and looked at Rick, talking while they walked along the hallway. "Does that put you on notice?" he asked.

"We knew she wanted to leave, and now she's looking for her next job," Rick stated. "Knowing what she can do for people in need, how could I possibly even stop her?"

"I didn't say *stop* her," Terk clarified intently, "but it would be nice if you two could sort out some personal issues before she leaves. It would make your recovery a whole lot easier too."

At that, Rick frowned. "I don't know. I seem to make it worse. This whole thing's a big mess."

"Only if you make it that way," Terk stated calmly. "Everything can be straightened out with clear communication."

Rick groaned. "Great. Thanks for that," he muttered. He turned around the computer room, checking if she had joined them here, when she walked in, her laptop in hand. She handed it over to Terk.

"Do your worst," she said. "I have no intention of accepting any work that will put me back into this scenario."

And, with that, she turned and walked back out again.

CHAPTER 11

CARA HAD BARELY reached the sanctity of her room when a knock came at her door. Knowing it would be Rick, she ignored him. When the door opened regardless, she turned and glared at him. "What's the point of knocking if you won't listen?"

"I couldn't hear any answer," he replied smoothly.

She tossed him a thunderous look and sat down on the edge of the bed.

"Listen, Cara, I'm really sorry that helping me has messed up your world."

"I'll get over it," she stated calmly. "I always do."

"Is it that easy?"

"No," she snapped, "it's not easy at all, but I can't let it completely destroy my life."

He winced at that. "I was hoping it wouldn't, and we're all very grateful. Especially me." At that, she stiffened, and, he was reminded once more how mentions of gratitude bothered her. "And you and I both know there's something between us."

"But we both also know that you don't believe anything is real about it."

"Is it common?" he asked. "You're the one with this very strange energy."

"It's not *strange* energy, except to you. I'm a healer.

That's all I do."

He took a deep breath. "I get that, but it seems like what you can do is a lot more."

"It's not," she repeated. "I'm a healer. That's all."

"Well, your healing abilities are pretty profound," he stated.

She gazed at him. "And?"

"I'm not comfortable with you leaving."

Her eyebrows shot up. "That's too bad. That attitude could make it difficult for you when I go."

He glared at her. "Now you're just being difficult."

"And you're not?" she asked.

He groaned, realizing they were just talking around in circles. *Again.* "I feel like, every time I talk with you, we don't quite get to the true matter. That's the problem."

"We don't," she agreed, "because you don't want to accept the reality of what is there."

"And what is that?" he asked specifically.

"Energy," she said, "but it's up to you whether you like it or not."

He frowned at that. "Meaning?"

"I forged bonds with you to save your life," she explained, "but, if those bonds make you feel like a prisoner, then obviously they're not good for you, and you must sever them."

He stared at her. "Not good for me? Is it that simple?"

"Not everything in life is simple," she noted, "but energy generally is. It's either good, or it's not."

"And would you say the energy between us is good or not?"

"Well, it certainly *was*," she replied cautiously. "What it is now is a whole different story."

"And why is that, do you think?"

"Because you're conscious again, so now you get to make decisions that you may or may not be terribly happy to make."

He took a deep breath. "And again it seems like we're talking in circles."

She laughed. "All of this stuff is fairly easy. It's all about communication. Either you want me in your life or you don't."

At that, he froze. "Wow."

She gave him a flat stare. "Wow what?"

"Are you saying that as a friend?"

She groaned. "I'm really not into people being that obtuse."

"Seriously? How could I possibly *not* be obtuse? An awful lot of information is flowing here that is new and different to me. Somehow I feel like I'm walking in a minefield."

"Only if you're the one who's putting down the mines," she replied candidly.

And he stopped. He realized what she was saying. He went to open his mouth, when another knock came at the door, and it was opened almost immediately.

Terk poked his head in. "Excuse my interruption, but with your last inquiry, they did send you medical records. Sorry for being intrusive about it, but it appears very suspicious."

"And why is that?" she asked him.

"Because I can't find the person they're asking for help with."

She frowned at that. "Can you always find everybody?"

"No," he admitted, "but generally, when somebody is

this broken, there would be a record of what happened to them."

"It should be in the medical file." She stared at him, frowning.

"But it's not," he stated clearly. "That's why I'm interrupting, to see what you would typically do next."

"Well, if I can't get full answers, it's absolutely no," she explained. "People don't understand the cost to me, and I also have to ensure that I can pay that price, depending on what is happening," she murmured, and got up. "Let me have a look at the email and the medical records."

Terk entered her bedroom, carrying her laptop.

She went through the medical records and shook her head. "No, these would not be sufficient for me to make a decision."

"Okay," Terk said, "so then what would you typically do next?"

"I would tell them no," she said quietly.

"Could you do that for me?" he asked. "Right now?"

Frowning, she did exactly that. "Does that help at all?"

"I'm not sure," he replied. "What it does do is give us a better idea of what they're doing. We're tracking that email, the IP address on it, and looking for scenarios with a patient like this," he shared.

"So you really think it's a fake job request? With a fake patient?"

"That's what I'm wondering, yes," he admitted succinctly. "I think it's a possibility."

She nodded. "I was surprised that the request was there, but I often find that a job is waiting for me, just after I've completed another one. So, timing wise, it was right on target. Yet I hadn't put out the energy to say I was looking for something else." She frowned at that. "So it caught me off guard, but it does happen that way every once in a while. … It didn't really raise any flags. However, I hadn't gotten to the point of doing an energy search for him either."

At that, Terk nodded, as Rick looked on. She saw the relief on Rick's face, and she smiled. "I don't just take on jobs without looking at it carefully, you know."

"And I'm glad to hear that," Rick stated, "because that would be way too easy for somebody to get to you. But, in this case, if there was no patient, you would know that, wouldn't you? Once you did your energy search?"

She nodded. "And I would be wondering what the hell they were up to." He hesitated, and she nodded. "Give me a couple minutes." She looked pointedly at Rick. "I need you to leave."

"And if I don't want to?" he asked. She glared at him. "Fine," he grumbled. "Can't you do any of this with people around?"

"I can," she admitted, "but it's easier if I have privacy."

And, with that, he stepped out.

IN THE HALLWAY Rick looked over at Terk. "She certainly wouldn't be easy to get along with," Rick noted.

Terk laughed. "And you are saying *she's* the one being difficult?"

At that, Rick stared. "No, I guess I'm not, am I?"

"You've been alone for a long time. You've been recently hurt. Your mind has been badly injured, and we're still in the midst of a terribly dangerous and traumatic situation," Terk noted. "So, at what point in time do you start to wonder if it's you and not her?"

"Ouch." Rick grimaced. "That doesn't sound very nice."

"No, it's not," Terk replied, "and yet what are your options right now?"

Rick looked at him. "That's what I was just trying to figure out with her. She says that I'm making it difficult, when it's really just a simple case of do I want her in my life or not?"

At that, Terk smiled. "Ah, communication. I really do like plain speaking, and she's right. She can remove all the energy. It will take a little bit of time, and it will possibly be painful for her."

"I don't want that," Rick stated. "I don't want to cause her any more pain."

"No, but if you don't feel the way she does, she'll have pain anyway."

At that, he stopped. "Can you explain that?" he asked. "Because nobody's really saying very much that I understand."

"That's because you're throwing up all these walls, trying not to see what's right there in front of you," Terk explained calmly. "That's always been a bit of an issue with you."

He groaned. "And, once again, I feel like I'm getting slapped down, but I don't know what I've done."

"Because you're not being honest with yourself, Rick. Do you like her?"

"I don't even know that liking her has anything to do with it," he argued in amazement. "It feels like she's a part of me."

"She is," Terk stated. "She's a major part of you now, but, if that is not something you're comfortable with, then she will do what's needed to remove that connection. She has never been somebody who wanted to hurt you or to make you feel like you were forced into this," he added.

"But is this like a friendship thing?" Rick asked cautiously.

Terk's laugh burst out, which was something Rick had almost never heard. "That," Terk said, "depends entirely on how much you want her in your life."

Rick let his breath out gently. "I want a lot more than what I'm really comfortable saying right now," he shared. "Because … I just don't know how much of it is gratitude."

"Come on, Rick. The gratitude went out the window a long time ago," Terk said, "back at the minute you judged her for saving your life in this way."

"I didn't mean to judge her," he replied. "It was just such a shock to find out about the governor. In fact, the more I hear about her skills, I am shocked yet again."

"Of course it was a shock, and, now that you've had some time, it's up to you to sort it out. And I mean *now* because, once she moves on, she's moved on," he declared. "She'll remove as much of that energy as she can, and, over time, she'll remove the rest of it, and she'll deal with the fallout on her own."

"What fallout?"

"If you care for somebody, and you're so close that you actually have that level of shared energy between you, what do you think the fallout is?"

With that, Terk turned and left.

CHAPTER 12

CARA STARED AT the ceiling. "What the hell is going on?" she murmured.

Was Terk correct? Was that what this was all about? Was somebody trying to get to Rick and to this whole group through her clients? It seemed like it could be true, but she just didn't know. She could sense the energy, but it didn't seem injured in any way, and, for someone like her, that would put all her flags on alert. It didn't necessarily mean that anybody else would agree with her. Terk would certainly listen, and he'd been the one to bring it up in the first place, so maybe he would believe her.

She wasn't sure about Rick. He was still riding the disbelief wagon, and, while it frustrated her, she really couldn't blame him. She'd thrown a lot at him in a very short time, but she had been pretty darn sure what was between them was real, but she also knew that, for someone like him, it would take a little longer.

She was okay with a little longer though, and, after their kiss, she thought they were getting somewhere, but now? Maybe not so much. It was also her fault for having fallen so deeply and being as affected by him as she had been. Sanity would say, *Pick up the pieces and run,* just so she could continue to do what she was doing to help multiple people. She didn't have a clue how she would even begin to help anybody if she was connected to this group though.

Tired and worn out, she got up and walked back to find everybody around the computer area, fussing away. "Did you find anything?" she asked.

Terk walked over. "The real question is, did you?"

"I found the energy, but definitely no injured person goes with it."

"And what do you think that would mean?" he asked.

"Somebody is playing games," she declared, "and I really don't appreciate games."

He smiled. "See? I knew we would always be on the same level."

"So, what will you do about it?"

"Actually I'm hoping you can help us find a location."

"I've never done any location work," she stated. "I couldn't even tell you where Brody was. Scott is a little stronger, a little closer to the surface, so there's some communication on an energy level there, but honestly? His sole focus is on this Naira."

Terk looked at her for a moment and then nodded. "That's also good to know, but you have Brody's energy signature, right?"

"I have what was there," she noted, "yes."

"Good," Terk replied. "We're trying to find a physical location for wherever this person is who is after us."

"He is close," she said.

Terk frowned. "Okay, we didn't even know that much. Can you tell me more?"

"I say that because I didn't have to use much energy to communicate. They're looking for a response from me right now. I would say that they're probably here in town."

"You can tell whether the energy is local or not?"

"Sometimes," she admitted. "In this case, because it's obviously not injured energy, it's a much stronger signature. They're close by. I'm sure of it."

"Good to know," Terk said. "They are probably preparing for an attack then."

"That would be my take," she murmured.

"Are you sure you don't want a job with us?" Terk repeated.

"I don't think so," she replied, with a smile. "You guys won't need as much healing as I normally offer."

"Did you always want to just heal?" Terk asked.

"It's what I do," she stated simply.

"And I get that," he murmured. "Do you have to physically be with the patient?"

"No, I don't," she said, "but it was always much more convenient to just move from one patient to the next, rather than trying to always deal from a second apartment and people who didn't understand."

"Right, so you did it knowing that people would ask less questions if you went to their site."

She nodded. "For the same reason, I always insist on complete anonymity and nobody can be around me while I'm working."

"And do people really let you do that?" Gage asked her.

"It's a condition of my work," she murmured. "If they aren't prepared for that much, they sure as heck aren't prepared for the rest."

He smiled at that. "That is a good point," he murmured. "I still think you should join the team."

"And again," she repeated, "you don't have enough work for me."

"I don't know. We keep getting injured," Gage replied,

with a smirk.

She laughed. "You know what? From that point of view, maybe so, but it's really not where my preferred work would be."

"Got it," Gage agreed, "but we'll still work on you to get you to change your mind."

She smiled. There was definitely a growing sense of acceptance with these people, and that was huge. She didn't even know what she wanted to do with her life right now because everything just felt so off. It was her own fault, but she was trying to disconnect from Rick, but, every time she tried, she ran into this damn resistance. She knew where it was coming from, but Rick had to make up his own mind. Still didn't answer the issue of her own future.

Just then a chiming sound came from one of the computers.

"He's here. He's here in Manchester," Tasha called out. "His email seems to have originated in London, but he's not there."

"So this is a setup then, by someone who's after me?" she asked, stepping closer to the computers.

A picture flashed up on the wall.

She stared at it. "Well, that's the one who contacted me, though that doesn't mean he's the one after you guys."

"And yet," Terk said, at her side, "what other connection would there be?"

"You guys have no doubt made more than a few enemies in your time"—she smiled—"so maybe that's for you to answer."

"I hear you." Terk gave a clipped nod. "Still, I'm pretty sure that this is one of the guys we were looking for."

Sophia agreed. "Yes, it is. I found some phone numbers

in common and a couple emails." She held up one finger. "Oh, hold on just a second." Her fingers flew over her keyboard. "Ha," she said a moment later. "I have an address."

With that, everybody spun to look at her.

"It's only about ten minutes from here," she murmured.

"Yes." Rick pumped his fist.

"I presume that means you want in on this one?" Terk asked Rick.

"Oh, hell yeah," he replied, his hand on his heart. Yet he felt a stillness beside him. Recognizing something odd going on, he spun to see Cara staring at him. "It'll be fine," he told her.

She shook her head. "No, it won't be."

Stunned, he asked, "What is it you're sensing?"

She looked at Terk. "Surely you're sensing it too."

He nodded. "Yes, I am." He looked at Rick. "And I presume there's no way we can convince you to stay back?"

"Hell no, not in this lifetime."

His wording brought an audible gasp from Cara.

His gaze locked on her. "Are you saying I'm in danger?"

She nodded immediately. "Yes, you are. They know about you. I'm not sure they know about the rest of the team, but it's you they are after."

"That's fine," he replied. "Then I'll take them out." He looked back at the others. "I'm assuming, as always, that the team will have my back?"

"We will," Damon agreed, "but are you sure about this?"

"I'm sure. I can't sit it out and let this fear do me in. And I get it. I understand that our best information suggests the possibility, or even the likelihood, of something very unpleasant heading my way," he murmured, "but, if you guys were in my shoes, I'm pretty sure you'd make the same choice."

Wade nodded, as did Cal and Gage.

"That's fine," Damon said, "but no Lone Ranger stuff. You've got to keep your cool."

Rick gave him a flat stare. "Who? Me?"

"Yeah, you," he drawled in exaggerated frustration. "We see it with you more than anybody else."

He shrugged. "No way, I'm a new man."

"Well, I don't know about that," Damon argued, "but you're definitely different."

With that comment still rattling around in his brain, and unsure what he should do with it, Rick turned to look at Tasha and Sophia at the computers. "Have you got the location up on the satellite?"

Tasha pointed at the screen. "While you guys were all busy, talking and chest-bumping," she teased, "we were working."

Just enough sarcasm filled her tone that everybody chuckled, as they came over and took a better look.

"It's not very far from that other house, where we found the dead guys," Damon noted.

"No, it isn't," Rick murmured, "and that's a good thing. The bad guys are probably keeping everybody close."

"Keeping them close is one thing." Terk studied the layout. "But how close is a completely different story."

They nodded but immediately started discussing plans.

Rick deliberately corralled the insecurities bouncing around inside him. This was not the time to get a case of nerves. As much as he wanted it to be a sure thing, there was no such thing in life, as the team all well knew. And this mission wouldn't be any different. When they finally had an agreed-upon plan in place, with Damon staying behind to manage communication central, and Terk on security watch, Rick, Cal, and Wade would go in. Gage would stay back since he'd been covering the latest security watch and needed some sleep so he could be of use soon.

Satisfied with that, Rick said, "Everybody be back in five, prepped and ready to go."

"We'll get the armory opened up," Terk stated.

Rick looked at him. "It's still hard to believe that this is where we're at now."

"Hey, I'm kind of liking it," Damon admitted. "I'd go for this long-term, as well."

At that, Terk looked at his team. "You've all said that several times now. We'll have to talk when we get back."

"Let's wait until we have the whole team," Damon suggested, "and that includes Brody. According to Cara, Scott could surface first and, with any luck, soon." With that, he turned his gaze toward Cara, and then Damon disappeared.

"Well, that was directed at me," she murmured.

"If you can keep an eye on our two members in the ethers while we're gone," Terk noted, "I could disconnect."

"Right," she agreed. "You'll need all your energy. Please keep Rick—all of them—safe."

"I will." He nodded. "At least I'll do my best. We might need your services, so please don't disappear."

She frowned. "You know I can't just be at your beck and call all the time, right?"

Terk smiled. "I get it. I really do. But, in this instance, I know that you'll be there. You and Rick haven't managed to get things sorted out yet," he murmured. "And you won't go far before you do."

"Yet I'd like to," she muttered.

"Yeah, you might," Terk noted, "but I also know that you can't."

She glared at him. "It's not nice to make fun of somebody who's struggling."

"You are the last person to be struggling with that." Terk gave her a wry look. "I know your heart is pure. Rick is just a little bit more of a slowpoke on these things."

"Yeah," she agreed. "I saw some of his history."

"Well, I wouldn't tell him that you know anything about *that*," he murmured. "At least not yet."

She nodded. "If he doesn't keep me in his life, I'll never tell him."

Terk smiled. "Give him some time. He's already there. He just needs to figure it out."

"Like hell he is *there*," she said, with feeling. "He's nowhere near ready."

At that, Terk laughed and headed away with the rest of the guys, as they each took care of their assigned duties.

Cara watched them go, with huge misgivings. She came up behind Tasha and Sophia at the computers. "Do you mind if I watch?"

"Not at all," they said together.

"We'll be keeping track of all their vitals on satellite," Tasha murmured.

Cara took her spot slightly behind them. "Is it always like this when they go?"

"When you're new, it probably feels like a lot of commotion," Tasha noted quietly. "Once you get accustomed to it, you realize they don't take unnecessary risks."

"But they're all angry right now, so how does that not interfere with their decision-making processes?" Cara murmured. "They're all upset."

"Of course they are upset. Wouldn't you be, if somebody you cared about was being targeted?" Sophia asked Cara.

Cara sighed, understanding fully how much caring for people carried real risks with it.

"Terk has been dealing with this since the attack that took them all out," Tasha explained. "By himself for a time, all while trying to keep every one of the guys alive, until they woke up. So, if you ever get any information on that initial bloody attack on the team, let us know." She added, "It took down more than just a few of us, and some went down for good."

Cara's eyes widened at that. "I get it, and I'll do what I can—but no guarantees that I find anything about the attack. That's so not my wheelhouse."

"That's the thing about life," Lorelei said, coming up behind her. "There are no guarantees in life, and still we do the best we can."

Cara knew for sure that she could do one thing, and that was to help Scott and potentially Brody, but she might need more help with Brody. With that decision made, she got up and went back to her room, where she focused her mind on reading energies. However, it was not just the two unconscious team members she wanted to keep an eye on. It was Rick. She knew that Rick was close to deciding on his future relationship with her, but he was still a long way from where she needed him to be.

She hadn't made the decision to help him lightly, and she was really hoping it wasn't a mistake, but it was coming down to crunch time. Even more so now that he was back out in the field, doing missions. If he could keep his focus and could keep his energy up, he would take the brunt of this mission, but she could do something to help minimize that, and, with that thought in mind, she proceeded to get some energy work done.

RICK FELT GOOD to have a weapon in his hand again. Nobody had even mentioned retesting to see if Rick was fit to carry one, and he appreciated that trust, since feeling like he was *less than* for the last few days had been rough. Now, with Wade and Cal beside him, they approached cautiously on foot.

Darkness was just falling, which gave them a perfect presentation of how best to approach this house. It looked completely innocuous, nothing different than any of the many other houses around them. Rick looked over at his two partners. "Are we really believing this is the address?"

"I would think so," Cal murmured.

"We certainly won't take a chance and not check it out. No reason not to trust Sophia's work," Wade added.

Rick agreed with that wholeheartedly, but it was a little hard to determine if this simple brownstone in the middle of a large piece of land had anything to do with the mess that they were working on. But he also knew that his team, these guys, every one of them, had come up against house after house, finding nothing but dead bodies.

Rick had been at the latest one, where they'd also come upon a curious neighbor, who was even now under protection, apparently something that Terk would have to pay for. Rick sympathized with everybody involved. MI6 was more than furious at the littering of bodies all around their country, but it wasn't Terk's team's fault, though nobody gave a crap about that.

Blame wouldn't be laid in a scenario like this, without other people feeling like something was going on that shouldn't be. Rick and his team were doing the best they could, but certain scenarios couldn't always be helped.

Having that weapon just made Rick feel like he was ready and more prepared than he had been up until now. Rick searched the surroundings. "I'm not sensing anything."

"Neither am I," Wade confirmed.

Cal added, "Keep your energy low, just in case."

"Just in case of what though?" Rick asked.

"We haven't figured out what they did originally to take us out," Cal murmured, "and, until we actually know what was going on, we can't take a chance of them attacking us like they did before, since we don't have anything in place to protect us."

Smiling broadly, Wade added, "Well, maybe you do, Rick, with Cara. Yet the rest of us? Not so much."

Rick shrugged. "I'm not sure what the deal is with Cara."

"Yes, you are," Cal argued. "You're just slow to acknowledge it."

Rick winced at that. "I gather everybody has an opinion."

"Everybody *always* has an opinion." Wade's soft laughter filled his voice. "What you don't realize is that we've all gone through this to a certain extent, one way or another, before you. You're just coming on board a little later than the rest of us."

"Right," Rick agreed, "and it feels like I'm behind."

"That's your insecurity talking," Cal noted. "We didn't all wake up at once and come back at full strength by any means. We came back one by one, each with different issues, all weaker than hell and all feeling the same way you are. Some handled it better than others."

Wade nodded. "So, you may be behind some of us, Rick, but you're not farther behind than Scott or Brody. When they surface, they will have a lot more to catch up on. Will you consider either of them late or less than?"

"Hell no. Okay, I get it," Rick said. "The sooner we're all back up and fully functioning, the better."

"But it takes as long as it takes," Wade noted. "Recovering from this can't be rushed. The stakes are too high."

"I was hoping that Cara would help Brody," Rick shared. "Scott sounds like he's doing much better, of the two of them."

"Well, I suspect she is," Wade said. "She probably doesn't want to make any promises that she can't keep."

"Plus," Cal reminded Rick, "while it appears she can do a lot, much of it still depends on Scott and Brody."

Rick nodded. "It must be hard to have those kinds of skills, knowing that, in the right circumstances, you can really help someone. But the other times? Realizing that some things just can't be fixed has got to be gut-wrenching."

"The other thing is," Wade added, "people are out there with a heavy need for somebody like her, and, once they discover her and her special skills, she becomes a target herself."

"Is that what you think is happening now?" Rick asked him.

"I don't know," Wade admitted. "It is something that I had to question because, in that scenario, she's in danger."

"I know," Rick agreed. "Terk was wondering if she was really the target, not me, back at the apartment we shared to heal me. It's possible certain people could be thinking that everybody on our team was alive because of her. And, if that were the case, she would become a huge target, and we don't want that to happen," Rick explained.

"No, of course not, and none of this is easy on any of us," Wade murmured. "None of us are back on our feet to the point that we can take on the whole world again. We do okay, but our stamina isn't what it should be by any means. And our abilities are all over the map compared to what they were. Some different, some stronger. We're having to retest and reassess everything."

Cal looked over at Rick. "I don't suppose she can do anything for us, can she?"

"I don't know the answer to that. How close are you to being back to full function?"

"Because of Terk, I'm doing as well as I am," Cal noted, "but I'll need weeks."

"Cara might be able to help," Rick replied. "I don't know what she might do versus what she's willing to do," he admitted, "and I really don't understand the part about how much it takes out of her."

"Strange to even think of any of that, isn't it?" Wade murmured.

"More than you can even believe," Rick shared. "It's sure not what I expected to wake up with, straight out of a coma."

"It's a really deep connection, isn't it?" Wade asked.

"It's incredibly deep," Rick murmured, "and yet, at the same time, it feels normal and natural, like it's been there forever."

"It probably has been," Wade stated. "At least, in her mind, she had to go pretty deep to do whatever she was doing, so I'm sure that connection spans a lifelong arc."

Rick added, "Maybe she can work on disconnecting, and it would be different. She'd still have the energy tied to me to a certain extent, but it wouldn't be anywhere near as intense."

"I don't know, dude," Wade replied. "I'd probably not go that route."

"Why not?" Rick asked Wade.

"Because I think it would always feel like you were missing a part of yourself."

Rick stopped and stared at his friend at that mention. "I hadn't considered that."

"Well, I wouldn't have either, if I hadn't discovered how great things could be with Sophia."

"Yeah, you'll have to fill me in on that at some point."

"Back to Cara," Wade said. "I know that you're more affected by her than you're quite willing to put out there right now—and I get that. I really do. I just hope you end up working it out. She's pretty special."

"Of course she's pretty special, but she needs to be special for other reasons than just her abilities," Rick argued.

Wade laughed. "And see? You would never have said something like that before. Not in a million years. All of us on the team were bemoaning not having someone, who could understand our gifts, even share them. And you know how rare a commodity we are. So finding partners so aligned to us? It must be an astronomical feat that the four of us, so far, have found someone. So I'm not buying that statement from you, buddy. You're running scared. And Cara's perfect for you."

Rick groaned. "It feels like there's this disconnect. There was *before*, and there's *now*."

"And that's exactly how it is," Wade agreed. "Why fight it? You obviously care."

Cal spoke up then. "I agree with everything Wade just said. You are looking a rare and beautiful gift in the mouth, my friend."

"I care, but is it real caring?" he asked. "I mean, after what I've been through and what she has done, is what I'm feeling for real, or is it just superficial—or something else entirely, like gratitude?" He shook his head. "I can't even describe it."

"Yeah, well, don't, … particularly when you're doing such a crappy job of it." At that, Wade's grin flashed again.

That simple act reminded Rick that everything going on between him and Cara was practically a public spectacle at headquarters. Not by his choice, but it was something he would really struggle with when this fact-finding mission into who attacked the team was over.

The sudden noise up ahead had the trio going silent. With hand signals, Rick and Wade neared the house, while Cal went wider into the trees. He was on perimeter watch and could jump in as needed. Rick and Wade shifted around to the side of the house, checking the windows as they went. Inside, one man walked around, talking on a phone, but they couldn't hear the conversation. That in itself was frustrating. With his face turned away from them, it was hard to also identify him.

As Rick watched through the curtain, hidden and still, he heard the man shout.

"No, it's not good enough, dammit. She's helping them, so we need to take her out. No, I'm talking about permanently."

At that, Rick's blood ran cold. He looked over to see

Wade's gaze harden as he too studied the scene he could see through that window. They didn't have any proof of who they were talking about killing, but, in his heart of hearts, Rick knew.

"You set it up, and you take her down," the man snarled into the phone. "I don't care how many others go at the same time, but you make sure she's done." After listening to the other person on his call, the yelling man added, "Jesus, there can't be any more of the team still up and running as it is. All eight were supposed to be done and gone. How the hell is this even something that's still up for discussion?" With that, he tossed his phone down onto the table, then walked over to the sideboard and poured himself a stiff drink.

Rick understood the feeling. The last thing he wanted was to have this guy wandering around, causing chaos with Cara. The team had to make sure that this was done tonight, but they also had to track whoever the hell it was who was taking the orders on the other end of the call.

Just then, another man walked into the kitchen. "Did you get a hold of Charlie?"

"I did. He doesn't agree with taking her down."

"What the hell?" he asked seriously. "I would have thought that was a given."

"Yeah, me too," he snarled. He tossed back his drink and looked at his partner. "What the hell's going on here anyway? We were promised that they would all be taken out permanently. Did they even get one? What a fucking mess."

"I know," his partner agreed. "We should never have sublet that job. That's the problem."

"Hell. It was sublet to us as it was," he snapped, "and they're on our case now too."

"Of course they are," he muttered. "The fact that anyone on the team is alive blows me away. The incompetence is another level altogether."

"That team must have help from somewhere. My vote is that woman. Trouble is, they've gone to ground, and I don't know where they are." He poured himself a second drink.

"Hey. Go easy on that stuff."

"Why?" he snapped. "This has all gone to shit, and you know it."

"How bad do you think it is?"

"I suspect we have a couple days, maybe a week," he murmured, "and then I wouldn't be at all surprised if there isn't a contract on our heads for failing to complete the job."

"Shit," he murmured. "That's not what I want to hear."

"It's the last damn thing I want to be saying," he added, "but you and I both know what happens if we fail."

"Well, failure wasn't supposed to be in the cards on this job." He stared at the other man. "How the hell did that even happen?"

"It's that bloody Terk and his team," he roared into the night. "Somehow they survived."

"I thought this was supposed to be cutting-edge technology. Sounds to me like it was a trial run, and they didn't know whether it would work or not, yet convinced you that it would."

"Oh. So I'm to blame now?" He shot his partner an ugly look.

"Hey, I'm not saying that at all. Calm down. All I'm saying is that we need to solve this, and we need to solve it now."

"If you've got any answers, fly at it," he spat. "Charlie is already telling me that taking out the woman will be too many deaths too quickly."

"Well, he has a point," the other man agreed cautiously.

At that, the first man spun on him. "Don't you start with me now. I've got enough on my plate without listening to that crap."

"I get it. You think that she had some ability to help them. I don't know where you got that idea, but, even if she did, if they're not around, she can't do a thing."

"Do you really want somebody out there who can heal people like she can?"

"Are you sure you haven't been dipping in that bottle a little too much?" he asked. "She's a nurse. That's all."

"Yeah, says you. I want her dead."

"I get it. I hear you. You want her dead, and you've already placed the order. So that's fine, but we can't keep doing this," he said. "If you find someone else who's trying to keep somebody alive, or doing whatever your head thinks they're doing, we can't just keep popping peripheral people. We're trying to take out *one group*. Those are the ones we need to focus on. Forget everybody else."

"I know the job. I get it, and I'm really not losing it. You know that, right?" He looked over at his buddy, as if seeking reassurance.

The second man nodded. "I know, man. We're all a little stressed and a bit overwhelmed right now. What was supposed to be a quick in-and-out job has turned into a complete FUBAR mission, and a lot of pain is to come if we don't solve this."

"A lot of pain is right," he agreed, "and not just for me. That'll be on you too."

At that, his friend stiffened. "How many people even know I'm involved in this?" he asked.

"Everybody. Do you think I didn't document this?" he asked. "Do you think I'll be the fool who gets left holding the bag at the end of the day? Hell no."

What happened next was almost preordained, but it was still shocking, as the second man pulled out a handgun and shot the first one at point-blank range, right through the heart. Rick and Wade stared at each other. What the hell? Had the reins of this whole nightmare changed hands, or were they now dealing with one less person and had something to rejoice?

Rick quickly sent a message to Terk about what had happened. Terk immediately cautioned them on quiet discretion, a reminder they didn't need. This was their job; … this is what they did.

It's just that they usually had more intel to go on, which was crucial, because, so far, this had ended up being a steady stream of bodies and very little forward progress. But they did know a little more than last time, and, with that intel firmly transferred to Terk, they swept around to the far side of the house to make sure no new arrivals were on scene.

Taking full advantage of the fact that the remaining guy was busy collecting all the incriminating materials in the house, preparing to make his escape, they slipped inside.

When the killer returned to the living room, he came to a dead stop because they stood in his face, each holding a gun on him. "Good God," he murmured. "He really was an idiot, wasn't he?"

"He really was," they murmured right back.

He shook his head. "I'm not quite so stupid."

"Considering you're disarmed at the moment and trying to get out of here," Rick noted, "we're not exactly sure who and what you are."

"Ah, so I finally ended up being somebody you don't know. Ha. I'm just the broker."

"Just the broker? Meaning what?"

"Meaning, I'm the one who parlayed one job into another. If I'd realized what a pain in the ass you guys would be, I'd never have gone in that direction."

"Then you didn't do your research," Wade noted, his voice hard. "Of all the things that we're known for, being a pain in the ass is pretty much a no-brainer."

"Yeah, of course. Nobody told me that ahead of time. So now what?" With his hands still up, he searched their faces. "We could make a deal," he murmured. "I'm quite open to that."

"I'm sure you are," Wade murmured. "The question is, what will we get out of it?"

"Names, dates, places." He shrugged. "I really don't care. I just want to get out of this. Obviously it's time for a career change."

"Are you that good at disappearing?" Rick asked him curiously. "You're connected to this mess, and, so far, anybody with a connection has been wiped out. Is the industry always that tough on its local hires?"

"It's not the industry," he stated. "It's this damn job."

"Yeah, well, that happens when you broker deals to kill people."

He shrugged. "That's what I always do. However, in this case, you guys ended up being a bigger pain in the ass than we had run across before."

"You want to explain just what's going on here?"

"Somebody wanted your team dead. We accepted the job, but pawned it off on another group to carry it out," he said. "I'm not even sure how many of your team are alive.

We collected half the money up front, and we were supposed to take payment for the rest afterward, upon proof of death—until they found out that Terk was alive. Terk was supposed to be taken out, but then somebody found out that another one of you was alive," he added. "Since then, it's just been this never-ending nightmare with more of you guys popping up all the time."

"And what about the attacks on the IT people working for us?"

"We were trying to flush somebody out in each case," he explained. "I don't even know all the details. I didn't want to know. As far as I was concerned, those guys we hired were supposedly pros and should have been able to do the job. Obviously I was wrong." He looked at Wade and Rick with a genial smile. "On the other hand, it's brought us to where we are now, gentlemen, and it sounds like it's your lucky day."

"In what way is it my lucky day?" Wade asked. "You better think hard before you speak right now because you two just sent somebody to kill a woman we care a lot about."

"Ah. But, if you had listened, you would have heard me say no."

"But the order has already been sent off," Rick stated quietly. "So how much is that *no* actually worth?"

"I can call it off," he said instantly. "I can tell him there's no money. That'll stop all of it."

"Now you've proven yourself to be a liar. Nice try. No, it won't. We've already seen that on this bloody mission," Rick replied. "There's always somebody trying to break into the business or to climb the ladder."

"Oh, that punk. *Sean.*" He brightened. "You must be the ones who took out him and his family. Thanks for that, by the way. Just entirely too many people were on this job, and I was getting very nervous. I've been making plans to get out of here myself for more than a few days now."

"Yeah, sounds like you have better survival instincts than these other guys do."

"I do," he agreed. "They put all their eggs in one basket and gambled on a new system that was supposed to stop you guys from ever doing whatever it is that you do. And believe me. I don't want to know," he stated. "Some things in life need to stay closed up in order to keep your sanity, and that is one of them."

"I agree with you there," Rick stated. "The problem is, you're already involved, and, if you're already involved, that's bad news for all of us."

"Nope, nope, nope." He shook his head. "It isn't … because I'm not involved. Like I said, I brokered the deal, that was it. Yet they kept screwing up, so I had to keep brokering more deals. Now you're here. It's all good. We can go."

"Go where?" Rick asked curiously. This guy clearly had an agenda. Rick didn't know what it was, but he didn't trust him, and he knew that in no way would Wade either.

"We need to leave here," the broker said, "because somebody'll be coming pretty damn fast."

"Yeah, and who's that?"

"Well, he already called in, looking for the job on that woman. Nobody does these deals without the money upfront anymore, so whoever it is my buddy called is coming to get the money."

"In that case," Rick noted, "I'm not going anywhere."

The broker laughed. "Don't be a fool. You could take him out even if you were blindfolded. You've been making idiots out of all of them this whole time."

"Hardly." Rick's tone was even harder than he expected. "You guys are the ones causing all kinds of chaos here. We need to get to the bottom of it and find out who's behind it all."

"So, if you're the broker, let's hear it," Wade snapped. "Who hired you?"

"I don't know who it was," he replied. "You don't really think we do names in this industry, do you?"

"Who put out this original nightmare contract?" Rick asked.

"Was it a new client?" Wade asked.

At that, the broker stopped. "Now that's a really interesting question," he murmured, as he studied Rick. "How about I let you have some information on the house, and the rest is for sale?"

At that, Rick immediately shoved his gun against the broker's head. "How about I let you have a few breaths of air, while I decide which is the best way to kill you?"

"Hey now, you really don't have to get difficult." The broker held up his hands in a placating manner. "I'm quite willing to share. I don't mind at all. It's not like I'll have anything more to do with this lot. At the same time, I really don't want to go down if I don't need to."

At times, this man was oddly honest, but it also made both Rick and Wade feel uneasy. Rick looked over at Wade, who was staring at the guy as if he'd come from Mars. *Right, that's exactly how I feel*, Rick told Wade telepathically.

"We come up against opportunists all the time," Wade murmured, "but not generally one this eager." Wade gave a quick glance to Rick.

"He's probably just trying to get out of Dodge, before anybody else finds out he's involved, and he's looking at us to do it for him," Rick suggested.

"Why the hell would we do that?" Wade asked. "He's the one who set up the hits on us."

The broker immediately shook his head. "I wish I could call them off. Really, guys. But, once the contract has gone out, it can't be rescinded."

"I don't know if we should even believe a word this guy says," Wade noted. "You know he's bound to be lying through his teeth."

"Why would I lie about something like that?" the broker snapped. "It would be in my best interests if I could call it off for you guys. I need you to get me out of here, free and clear."

"And why would we do that again?"

"Because I can give you all kinds of information," he repeated.

"But nothing you've given us so far leads us to believe you've got anything the least bit helpful. If you can't call off the contract, and you won't tell us who hired you, what good are you?" Rick replied in disgust.

"Well, I do know about lots of other contracts that I put in place," the broker added. "Now that they know that you're alive and well, they're out there hunting for the rest of your team."

At that, Wade stiffened. "And who are they hunting?"

He frowned. "I'm not sure. I think his name was Brody or something. They are close to running down his location, I think."

"Says you," Rick countered, with a negligent shrug. But inside, he felt the panic rising at the thought of Brody being helpless somewhere and these assholes finding him.

"Yeah, yeah, yeah." The broker shook his head. "I know

you guys are all big and tough, but you're still humans."

"You've already said you can't stop the contract."

"No, but, if you know ahead of time, you could get this guy somewhere safe."

"Sure," Rick muttered, "but that would mean we'd have to trust you, and all you're doing right now is setting us up for a trap. How about giving us some names instead?"

At that, the broker smiled. "You know what? That's a very good idea. Let's see how this would work. I would give you a name. You would tell me that it's no good. You would come back and say you want more. I would tell you another name. You would tell me the same thing." He sneered. "Pretty soon, you would think you've got everything there is to know from me, and then you would shoot me."

"Does it look like we're in the business of shooting people?" Wade asked.

"You and I both know you're in the business of shooting people," he stated, his tone hard. "You've left a pretty good string of bodies around the city lately."

"Nope." Rick looked over at Wade, seeing the look of disgust on his friend's face. Rick knew that Wade was of the same mind as he was. "No deals, but I'm sure MI6 will be interested in hearing what you have to say."

At that, the other man stopped. "Whoa, whoa, whoa. No need to bring them into this. I'm sure I can provide you with everything you need."

"I'm sure you could try," Rick noted, "but that doesn't mean we can trust anything that comes out of your mouth."

At that, the broker somehow managed to look like they'd injured his pride in some way. "Hey now, no need to insult me."

"We just watched you shoot your partner," Wade stated

calmly. "That tells us everything we need to know."

"No, no, no, wait, guys. You just didn't understand what you were seeing. Obviously he was off his rocker and would be a major headache. That can't happen here. You know that. We have more than enough headaches going on right now already."

"Yep, no lie there," Rick agreed. "All the local hires are dead, as you mentioned earlier. But here's a news flash. We didn't kill 'em. They were killed on authority of whoever did the hiring. Probably through *you*, the broker. So how many are actually on these contracts?"

The broker's eyes widened at that scoop. "Well, the problem is, the original contract is still open. We were given a deposit, but, so far, job satisfaction wasn't completed. So, I know that they're looking for the rest of your team to make sure they are really dead. And, of course, the fact that you are standing in front of me is a problem." He shrugged. "You should be dead already."

"Give us everything you can, about whomever it is who posted this job."

His lips twitched. "Wow, I would have thought you guys already knew it."

At that, they looked at each other, then at him with a hard gaze. "What does that mean?"

"It's just, I had assumed that you guys had all these answers and that you already know who has your back and who doesn't," he said.

"Are you saying it's our own government?" Rick asked.

"You guys really don't trust anybody either, do you?" A look of feigned innocence filled the broker's gaze.

That sent Rick's back up. And was likely a response to Wade's comment about the broker shooting his own partner.

Maybe they deserved the comment coming back to bite them; Rick didn't know, but they wouldn't get caught up in any games with this one.

"We'll let Terk decide," Wade murmured. "Come on. Let's get him out of here before somebody else shows up."

"You take him back. I'll stay here and make sure I catch this asshole who's after Cara," Rick said.

"Cara, yes, that was her name," the broker confirmed, with a knowing nod. "I figured you guys would probably know who they were talking about."

"Yeah, we know who they're talking about," Rick admitted, "but so do you."

"Hey, I just pay the bills." He gave a wave of his hands. "And I'm glad not to have to pay this one." He shot a look down at the dead man on the floor.

"Maybe, but there'll be payment due of some kind," Rick noted calmly. "There always is."

He winced. "Isn't that the truth? You know that, even when you think you're in the clear, you're not. Keep that in mind, gentlemen."

Just then Wade's phone buzzed. Wade pulled it out and took a look. "Terk is on his way."

"Good," Rick murmured. "We can get this settled fast."

"It won't be fast enough." The broker stepped forward ever-so-slightly.

"Hold your ground." Rick held the gun against the broker's head.

"Or what?" he asked.

"Or I'll shoot," Rick told him. "I've just come back from the dead. I really don't give a shit."

"What do you mean, back from the dead?" he asked in fascination. Then his face lit up. "Oh. You're one of the team members they didn't expect to make it."

Rick just ignored him, interested in what he might reveal.

"Wait. How the hell did you make it?"

Rick shook his head. "Wouldn't you like to know."

"Unless, of course, it *was* that woman, in which case she is way more valuable alive than dead." He looked down at his buddy on the floor. "What kind of an idiot are you?" he asked. "Something like that? Wow. She would be worth an incredible amount of money."

Rick felt his stomach churning at the thought of this asshole taking out somebody so pure and beautiful as Cara, just because they were scared of what she could do and didn't want her helping the people they were trying to kill. He wasn't sure which was worse, that scenario or selling her to the highest bidder. "Too bad it won't happen then, huh?" Rick asked.

"You mean, you hope it won't." The broker smirked. "I told you the orders already went out."

"And you can't shut them down. So what good are you?" Rick asked.

"Right. I can't shut them down." He shrugged. "And you know that already, so we can keep going around and around this circle, or you can help me get out of here and let me help you, as I told you that I would."

"Yeah, you say that, but you haven't given us anything of value yet," Rick replied. "So, I want to know exactly who your good dead buddy here called and who we're looking for that's coming after Cara?"

"Cara," he repeated in that soft voice. "Such a nice name."

Rick stepped forward, even as he heard Wade behind

him, warning him to stay calm.

"Just take it easy, Rick."

"Hell no. Why should I?" Rick asked. "This guy is nothing. A bullet is all he deserves."

"Yeah, but, just because that's what he deserves, it doesn't mean that's what he gets."

Unfortunately that was just too damn true, and Rick was pretty damn tired of these scumbags walking away with absolutely no repercussions. He looked down at the body on the ground, then up at their prisoner and smiled at Wade. "I'm thinking MI6 will want this guy."

"Well, maybe they do," the broker agreed, "but you won't let them have me."

"I don't know," Wade countered. "That probably would be the best answer. Let them deal with him. Either they can protect him or they can pull information from him. I don't care what they do with him."

Rick nodded. "Yeah, that'll be Terk's call."

"Fine, but he sure as hell needs to get here fast because I don't like anything about this wait," Wade noted.

"Smart," the broker said, with a smile, "because you know what they're like."

Rick added, "I know that they kill off everybody who's been involved, so, if you're still alive, they'll be looking for you."

"I pay the bills." The broker smirked. "Nobody's taking me out."

"You mean, you hope not," Rick stated calmly. "Like I said, *everybody* has been taken out so far."

"Yeah, but not the one who signs the paychecks," he murmured.

There was some potential truth to that. "In that case,"

Rick noted, "sifting through your life should be fun. We might find all kinds of stuff."

"You won't find a thing," he murmured. "Do you think I'm an idiot?"

"Well, if you're asking, then yes," he replied calmly. "I do. The fact of the matter is, you shouldn't even be here. And the fact that you are, that says a lot."

"It does," the broker agreed. "It says I'm the last man standing."

"Are you though?" Rick asked, with a smile. "Because, if you are, then we definitely want to keep you for some questions."

He smiled. "I told you that I'm useful."

The trouble is, Rick didn't trust him, not at all. He also knew that, if he didn't trust him, chances are nobody else did either. Including his own team. "Another reason for the higher-ups to kill you, don't you think?"

The broker seemed to be holding his breath.

"Was it your order that had the second group taking care of the contract?" Wade asked.

"Well, I was overruled. Again I pay the bills. I don't make the final decisions," he said apologetically.

At that, Rick nodded. "I've seen that before too," he muttered. "They put idiots in charge of this stuff and expect them to know what they're doing."

"Right," the broker said in disgust. "I've never seen the kind of muck ups this group had."

"I'm surprised they were still using them."

"Somebody else is pulling the strings," he noted.

"What are you supposed to do then?"

"I don't know," he admitted, "but it sounds like somebody messed up big time—but it goes back to this software that they thought would handle your team. Now they're cleaning up their mess."

"You could tell us where they're from at least."

"Iran," he shared, "but that won't help you much."

But it was a good tip. It was the confirmation that they needed. Rick nodded. "Actually it's a big help. Thanks for that."

"You're welcome. I told you that I can cooperate," he said agreeably. "You just have to keep me alive."

"That is a bit of a problem in your world," Rick stated, "because the big boss men keep killing off you guys."

"I think there's somebody else with a secondary contract. A fail-safe cleanup contract."

"And were you part of that, acting as broker?" Rick asked.

"No," the broker replied. "That's the problem, and I'm a little worried about that." He tapped his head. "I mean, I knew it was a possibility, which is why I was trying to get out, to get my plans in order, and to disappear. I wouldn't even be here today normally. Sounds like I should have listened to my gut on that."

Rick looked around and swore. "Isn't it awfully quiet out there?"

"It is," Wade agreed. "Too damn quiet."

"Shouldn't you be checking it out?" the prisoner asked hopefully.

Rick looked over at the pencil pusher, who had absolutely no compunction about pulling the trigger on his partner when it was time, and smiled. "I don't know. Might as well wait until they come in here."

They could see the broker getting noticeably nervous. "You don't understand what these guys are like," he whined.

"Maybe you should tell me more then, *before* they blow out your brains," Rick suggested.

The broker glared at him.

"Give me something, as a good-faith bargaining chip."

"Like what?" the broker asked, clearly tempted.

"Where in Iran?"

He named the same location where Terk's team had supposedly killed all of an Iranian team—the ones trying to duplicate Terk's team, but for use on the side of evil.

"Group name?"

He hesitated, then shrugged. "You already know the leader's name. That group took the job at a cheap price because they wanted to test this great new weapon they had, and they were looking at going after you guys anyway. So it was supposed to be a two-for-one deal. But unfortunately neither worked."

"Ah," Wade murmured, "in that case, maybe you do have something to offer."

"I don't know much about them," the broker added. "We were waiting for the final proof that the job was done before I paid them," he murmured, "but there could be this other contract that didn't use a broker."

"Wow. You could be gunned down for not completing the job, even if you subbed it out. And, if you didn't pay the other guys, the ones you subbed the job to," Rick noted, "you know they're coming after you."

"Well, they were doing it cheap anyway," he noted. "It was a test run. We were hoping it would work and thought it did for quite a while. Then the rumblings and rumors began about some of you being alive. Once we knew it definitely hadn't worked, well, what can we say? We have to finish the damn job," he stated. "Yet I won't pay the subcontractors for a partial job."

"No, and you're not getting the down-payment money back either," Rick agreed, "and you'll—"

A *pop* sounded, and the back of the broker's head exploded. Swearing, Wade and Rick ducked for cover, but it was too late for the broker. He toppled over slowly, complete shock on his face. The broker hadn't seen it coming.

Wade was still swearing up a blue streak. "Goddammit, they're always just that step ahead."

"We should have seen them coming," Rick murmured.

Wade nodded. "We understood we had a couple bad guys coming our way, wanting to get paid."

"Maybe that's what triggered this now."

And, sure enough, a birdcall came from outside. Terk and his brother both raced inside, heading for cover.

"Jesus," Merk said, when he saw two more dead bodies on the floor. "I gather they saw us coming."

"Yeah, I would take that as a yes," Wade noted quietly, "and, once again, they're cleaning up."

"This guy, he's the accountant, aka the broker," Rick explained, "and we were just getting to some interesting answers."

"And they took him out, right?" Terk asked.

"Right," Wade confirmed, now checking out each guy's pockets, getting what IDs he could find and snapping pictures of them. "MI6 will want them, and we'll need to tear apart their lives."

Rick nodded in agreement. "Send the information to Tasha and see if they can get a start on it. Have Lorelei look through what she can access too. We need to get what we can," Rick snapped, "and we need to get back. They are after Cara."

Wade looked over at Merk, who said, "Get going. Go, go, go. I'll cover you."

And, with that, Rick and Wade met up with Cal, and they raced out under the cover of Merk's fire, then bolted into their vehicle and headed for home. Almost immediately, as they neared the warehouse, Rick felt his instincts kicking in. He looked over at Wade and Cal, asking them, "Are you guys getting a bad feeling about this?"

Wade looked at him in surprise, then frowned. "Now that you mention it."

"Yep, me too," Cal confirmed.

And Rick slammed the gas pedal to the floor.

CHAPTER 13

CARA HAD ALREADY done as much as she could and was bored, struggling to keep her mind occupied, even as she monitored Rick and tried to keep a watch out on Brody, whose energy was quiet. Rick's energy flashed with stress, but he was holding. Until suddenly he wasn't. She sensed … something but didn't know what.

Mariana finally said, "Maybe you should help me cook."

"Maybe. It's just such a strange thing to be waiting and feeling like something is wrong."

At that, she looked at her. "Is that how you feel?"

"Yes," Cara said.

Mariana looked at her and asked, "Are you getting an ugly feeling?"

At that, Lorelei stepped in. "I am," she announced.

The women looked at each other.

"And Cal is with Rick?" Mariana asked.

Lorelei nodded. "And Wade. And it just feels wrong." Immediately she pulled out her phone and started to text him. "I don't know where they are, but I'd feel better if they were here."

"Maybe," Cara murmured, as she stared out in the distance. "There's definitely …" She shrugged, as she looked at the others. "Energy moving around, and please, don't ask for any more details than that."

"In a negative way?"

"Yes, absolutely." She nodded. "Something is wrong." As she frowned, she turned and surveyed the space around them. "How safe are we here?"

"Since they set up the perimeter guards, very safe," Lorelei stated.

Cara looked over at Mariana. "Where is Little Calum?"

Immediately she disappeared, only to return moments later with relief on her face.

"He's still napping on the couch," she stated.

Cara added, "Keep him with you. I don't like anything about this." And, with that, Mariana left to be with her son. Meanwhile Cara headed to Tasha and Sophia, who were back at the computers. As Cara neared them, she asked, "Has there been any change on the outside security system?"

Both women frowned at her, then checked the monitors. Tasha replied, "No. Why?"

"There will be," Cara said, and, almost instantly, a cacophony of alarms went off.

"Jesus," Sophia replied, looking over at her. "You're good."

"Well, if I was good," she noted, "we wouldn't be in this position." She looked around. "Weapons?"

"Yes." And, with that, Tasha hopped up and raced off to the nearby closet. "What can you handle?"

"Anything you give me," she stated calmly.

Tasha looked at her in surprise, handed over the pistol she held, and asked, "Can you really fire these?"

"I don't need to fire them," she explained. "For me, it'll be a prop." At that, with her jaw set, and leaving the other woman stunned, she immediately took up a position behind the front door.

Tasha and Sophia exchanged a glance and immediately raced to hide. They had weapons at the ready as well.

"So, we have a security system set up, and that's what the alarm is from?" Cara asked them.

"It's been infiltrated," Tasha noted. "Some other system is blocking it."

Cara tilted her head, concentrating. "I've got it mostly blocked, but it's like a high-pitched, ear-piercing scream."

"Oh, Jesus," Tasha murmured. "We've had some trouble with those before. It was absolutely horrific."

"It is, and it's about to drop some people in here," she warned them, looking around. "If you don't have ear protection, you need to get something now."

With that, the women raced into the closet again, searching for any ear protectors they could use. Because of the other attack, there were some in stock, and, as soon as they had their ears covered, and a set distributed to Mariana and Little Calum, they returned to the computer room, looking to her for guidance.

Cara shrugged. "Just hide and wait for it."

Within minutes, the sound split the air. All the women, even within ear protectors, bent over, but, in Cara's case, she put an energy shield around her head and kept it there as firmly and as solidly as she could. She knew what this would do. It would drop everybody to the ground, and that's when the intruders would enter, and she didn't dare let anybody in.

Not when so many potential victims were here, particularly Little Calum. The women here were capable, of course, but no match for these ruthless killers. These assholes didn't give a shit who they hurt, but no way in hell would anybody get past Cara to hurt a child.

The door burst open with a suddenness that shocked her, even though she expected it. She waited, as a machine gun appeared first. Almost instantly a handgun came up next, as a second man entered. She waited, her gaze on them as they slowly entered the room. They were probably expecting to see people on the floor, and instead everybody was hidden and struggling to stay conscious, even through the insufficient ear protectors.

When the gunmen turned and found her, she smiled and immediately dropped her shield to reach out and plow the closest intruder with an energy jolt that should have had him dropping to the floor. He didn't go quite flat to the floor, but he sank to his knees.

She had been forced to put the shield right back up in order to block out the horrific noise again. Beside the first gunman, the second gunman turned in surprise, and she used his own weapon to buck up against his chin. This caught him off guard, frozen, as he stared at her in shock. Her knee to his groin bent him over quickly. She followed up her attack on the first gunman by using a back kick to knock him to the floor.

With that, the other women came in, with guns raised, and stopped the intruders. The men dropped their weapons in disgust, but the stupid sound still raged on. Cara immediately removed the gunmen's ear protectors and tossed them to the women. The men cried out, dropping to the ground, curled into fetal positions, trying to protect their ears.

With the ear protectors designed to counteract this sound now worn by Sophia and Tasha, they approached Cara.

Shouting over the noise, Cara asked, "You know how to shut it off?"

Tasha immediately raced over to the computer. Suddenly all was silent.

Cara looked at Tasha. "Did you do that?"

"No, I think Gage and Damon are back," she replied.

Just then, the rear door burst wide open, and many men entered, but they were their men.

Cara looked at Rick and smiled. "About time you got back." Instantly she was plucked off her feet and hugged, as Rick threw his arms around her and held her close. She buried her face in tight against his chest. "That noise was awful," she moaned.

He nodded. "It's doing what it's meant to do." He looked down at the men on the ground. "Did they hurt you?"

"No, I didn't give them a chance."

He noted the weapon she still held. "Do you know how to use that thing?" He stared at it and looked back at her.

She gave him a flat stare. "I didn't need to use it. It's more of a prop than anything."

"We'll teach you," he stated, "because anytime you pick up a weapon, you need to know how to fire it."

"I would have figured it out," she replied. "Generally I don't need weapons like that."

Tasha nodded. "You should have seen her drop-kick those guys."

"So where did you learn self-defense?"

"Growing up," she said. "It just made my life a little easier when there was unwanted attention."

He snorted with laughter at that. "You, lady, are dangerous."

She smiled. "Only to the wrong person," she murmured.

"I hear you there, and I'm grateful I'm not on the wrong

side."

She tilted her head and stared at him. "Are you sure?"

He chucked her under the chin. "I'm positive. I might be slow. It might have taken me a while, … and mostly, because I felt like the choice had been taken from me," he murmured, "but I don't stay stupid for long."

She grinned. "I don't know about that part. I figured it might take you a little bit longer to figure it out."

"Nope, won't take me very long at all." He bent over and kissed her passionately. He looked around at the rest of the guys, all staring at them. "Can you guys handle the rest of this? Cara and I have a few things to sort out." And, with that, he scooped her up into his arms and carried her to her room.

She protested in the hallway, until Terk reached out, grabbed ahold of her handgun, and said, "You won't be needing this."

"You're right," she agreed. "I don't need any weapons for this guy." She snorted.

Rick laughed, as he closed the door behind him. "I'm glad you feel that way because you know that I'd never hurt you, right? At least not intentionally."

She stopped, looked at him. "I know that."

He searched her gaze and, apparently satisfied, nodded.

She smiled. "Besides, I wouldn't let you."

"I do like a woman with confidence." He chuckled.

"I mean it," she repeated. "My mother was an abused wife, so no way in hell would I ever let myself become part of that same scenario."

"Good. No woman should ever have to fear for her life at the hands of somebody who supposedly loves her," he said in disgust. "But it happens more often than a lot of people realize."

"Too damn often," she murmured.

He wrapped his arms around her and held her close. "I didn't get it at first. I started to feel like something was wrong later."

"It came on very quickly," she murmured. "I think because you guys have so many protective measures in place that I couldn't get any of the energy I needed as a warning system."

"Well, we'll have to work on that," he noted.

She looked up at him. "How did it go for you?"

"Well, we found the guy who was supposedly trying to hire a hit on you. His buddy shot him, but he'd already managed to get a call out to reaffirm his intentions. But, as Terk and his brother arrived, the broker's own cohorts blew his head off. So, once we figured out what was going on," Rick explained, "we offloaded the dead guys on poor Merk and came back here."

"MI6 will not be happy with you," she murmured.

"Probably not," Rick agreed. "Do they know about you?"

She just gave him a look.

"Will you ever fully share who and what you are?" he asked gently.

"One day"—she shrugged—"but it's really not that mysterious. It's just that more than a few people know what I can do, and, when it suits them," she noted, "they call me."

He nodded. "Got it. I really am grateful to you for saving my life."

She shrugged.

"And I know you don't want to hear gratitude, but it needs to be said. It took me a while to figure out the reason why I was so distrustful. Remember when I woke up, and I asked you if anybody had been in my sickroom?"

She nodded.

"And you said no."

Cara smiled at him and explained, "I knew people had been there, and I told you that it was Terk, but on an energy level."

"Sure, but that was a bit more than I could believe at that time," Rick added, "and I wasn't exactly seeing or understanding what you could do," he murmured quietly. "And it was a bit much, so I always had this little bit of distrust about it all."

"And now?" she asked, looping her arms around his shoulders.

He dropped his head, so their foreheads rested together. "Now I get it," he replied. "When you said we were joined, I thought you just meant energy."

"I did," she said in surprise.

He nodded. "But that energy has entered at a level that I had no idea was possible," he murmured, "and, because I didn't understand it, I didn't trust it."

She nodded. "You'll be one of those who has to see everything for himself, won't you?"

"Well, I didn't think so. I mean, Terk has certainly helped me get over some of that." He chuckled. "But I can see how it looks from your perspective." He reached down and kissed her. "And now I do understand. I can feel it myself. It's inside our hearts."

"That's what happens," she stated. "With something like that, you have to actually feel it in order to have that level of healing over somebody. In order to feel, I have to surrender. In order to surrender, you do too," she murmured. "And what ends up happening is that we bond on a level that most people never achieve in their entire lifetimes."

He held her close. "I've always been a bit of a loner," he murmured, "so it all just seemed very strange to me."

She chuckled. "What about now?"

"Now it feels normal. It feels natural, and unfortunately it also feels like, if anything ever happens to you, I'll probably have to kill myself," he murmured.

She shook her head. "Nope, what you don't realize is, at this level, even if I am not on this planet anymore, I'll still be in your heart. I'll still be there. I'll still be part of your soul. You can't get rid of me that easily."

He held her close, overwhelmed, and she just cuddled him, feeling the tremors in his body.

"It's okay, you know?" she said. "I get that it's new, but it will become something you become quite happy with."

"I get it. Mostly," he murmured gently. "I'm almost there."

"No, you are there," she argued. "Otherwise you wouldn't have come racing back."

"You knew I was coming, didn't you?"

"Sure," she agreed. "I wasn't really trying to hurt those guys. I just wanted to keep them from hurting anyone, until some of you guys got here to deal with it."

"Yeah, it looked like we all got here at once."

"Interesting how you so casually tossed off dealing with those gunmen onto your team."

He chuckled. "Hey, I had more important things to do."

"And what was that?" she asked, her eyes wide.

He lowered his head and whispered, "This," and kissed her with renewed understanding.

When he lifted his head, she murmured, "We really should be lying down on the bed for this." But she already was. She laughed out loud, wrapped her arms around his neck. "Oh, you're good."

"I'm glad," he whispered, "but you're much better."

When he lowered his head this time, their passion overtook them at a speed she'd never experienced before. Their clothes were tossed to the side, and, before she realized what was going on, he was already at the entrance to her body.

He whispered, "Let me in."

"Come on home." She smiled against his lips. She opened herself up, letting him slide deep inside.

He groaned and shuddered in her arms, as he struggled for control, but she didn't want him to have it. She wanted him to lose that control and to just show up 100 percent right now. She reached down between their bodies and gently stroked him. He immediately shattered and thrust hard and deep. By the time he reached for one more thrust, she was already arching into the next one. She cried out, and, by the third one, had already exploded in his arms. She dimly remembered him coming soon afterward, before he collapsed beside her.

"Wow," she murmured.

"Yeah, I'll say," he whispered, holding her close.

"If I'd realized that was waiting for us, I might have pushed you a little harder," she murmured.

He burst out laughing. "I don't know about that. I had to get to this on my own."

"Yeah, and you're definitely a little on the slow side."

He snorted. "I promise I'll pick up speed now."

She grinned. "Don't change, Rick. You're exactly the way you're meant to be."

"And how is that?"

"The other half of my soul." And she wrapped him up in her arms and just held him close.

EPILOGUE

S COTT WOKE UP. His gaze was fuzzy, his eyes ached, and he didn't recognize anything around him. The woman sleeping in the chair beside him though, that was someone he knew. He blinked several times to be sure. "Naira?"

She bolted to her feet and raced to his side. "Hey. How are you?"

He drifted back under without answering; just knowing that she was here was incredible. It felt like he'd been climbing through the clouds to get back to her for a very long time. There was another woman though, a woman whose named evaded him, and that bothered Scott because he felt like she was important, and he didn't know who or how she fit into things, but Naira was here, and that mattered in a way that he couldn't even explain. He heard voices dimly in the background, and he tried hard to focus, but he couldn't.

Another voice whispered in his consciousness. *Relax. You've made the big jump. Now just calm down and rest.*

Scott kept fighting toward consciousness, and, when it wouldn't work, he felt himself panicking. A gentle touch reached out, stroked his forehead, and he was out cold.

When he woke the next time, a frown was on his heart. He didn't know what was going on, but more awareness was slowly returning. Had he just dreamed that Naira was here?

He opened his eyes, and, sure enough, she sat at his bedside again. He stared at her. "What are you doing here?"

And damn if his voice didn't sound like it was rocks in the water, gravelly and yet soft.

She bounced to her feet. "Terk told me that you were here and that you were hurt."

Scott noted a little nervousness in her voice and her gaze. He closed his eyes again. "You're not supposed to be here."

"I know," she admitted in a low voice, "but I couldn't stay away."

He tried to open his eyes, but, once again, he went under.

When he woke the next time, he was alone, and he hated to say it, but it was a relief in itself. He wasn't sure what he had seen before, but no way Naira should have been here. She was married, with a husband and a whole different life, one that didn't include Scott. He rested for a moment and then slowly shifted in the bed, searching, looking around. He didn't know where he was.

Almost immediately the door opened, and Terk stepped in, along with another woman. Thankfully it wasn't Naira. Scott wouldn't mention Naira's presence either, since it would show where his mental state was, and he couldn't afford that. The woman stepped forward, placed a hand on his forehead, and he determined she was a nurse, although she didn't wear the traditional scrubs.

She smiled at him. "My name is Cara. How are you feeling?"

He stared up at her, feeling a recognition that he didn't quite understand, but he nodded. "I think I'll live."

"Good." Terk stood beside him. "We've been waiting a long time for you to come back."

Scott stared at his old friend. "How long?"

"Over a month," Terk replied. "A few days longer, I guess."

Scott's gaze widened. "I've been out that long?" he asked in alarm.

Terk nodded. "And you'll slowly recover. You know what happens when your body has been incapacitated for that long. It'll take some time to recuperate."

"Well, I'm sure you probably have some magic juice to help me get back on my feet faster," he murmured. "The nightmares are the worst." He shook his head. "God. It's almost enough to stop me from going back to sleep."

"We can't have that." Cara stood at his side. "Rest is what you need, and rest is what you'll get."

Something was in her tone. He looked at her. "As long as you don't do anything to force me back to sleep again because I've had some of the roughest nightmares ever."

"Not at all," she replied gently, "but you do need to rest, and you do need to sleep."

"Maybe." He yawned, looked around. "Where's everyone else?"

"Most of the team are back on their feet," Terk noted. "I hate to say it, but you're one of the last few to surface."

He stared at him. "Seriously? Even as strong and fit as I was?"

"You also took part of that blast a little harder than anybody else."

"I don't even remember what happened." But he felt the need to sleep taking over again. "I'd go back to sleep right now but for those damn dreams."

Immediately Cara put her hand on his forehead and said, in a gentle voice, "Sleep."

And just before he lost consciousness, he whispered, "Was she here?"

"Was who here?" Terk asked, his voice low.

He whispered, "Naira. Was she here?"

Scott waited desperately to hear the answer, only to go under—the question left unanswered.

This concludes Book 5 of Terkel's Team: Rick's Road.

Read about Scott's Summit: Terkel's Team, Book 6

Terkel's Team: Scott's Summit (Book #6)

Welcome to a brand-new series from *USA Today* best-selling author Dale Mayer, where dark-ops SEALs have special senses and skills, needed to solve intrigue, betrayal, and … murder. A series with all the elements you've come to love, plus so much more, … including psychics!

Everyone has the right to make a mistake, … but the one Naira made isn't one Scott can forgive. He wakes from a coma, sure that the ex-love of his life had been at his side, but finds no sign of her. When he does see her, he can't get past a long-ago decision she'd made that tore them apart.

Naira had hoped that Scott would protest her decision way back when, but he didn't say anything to stop her. Heartbroken, she went ahead with the business marriage to appease her father, which ends in divorce. When Terk called, she came running to Scott's bedside, even knowing he'd hate to see her when he woke up. But she has always loved him and can only hope he might find his way back to her.

But finding his way back to the team is on his mind,

with Naira second. Except that the operatives who took down his team initially are coming around and trying to pick off everyone left alive—and all the people they hold dear, … like Naira.

Find Book 6 here!
To find out more visit Dale Mayer's website.
https://geni.us/DMTTScottUniversal

Magnus: Shadow Recon (Book #1)

Deep in the permafrost of the Arctic, a joint task force, comprised of over one dozen countries, comes together to level up their winter skills. A mix of personalities, nationalities, and egos bring out the best—and the worst—as these globally elite men and women work and play together. They rub elbows with hardy locals and a group of scientists gathered close by …

One fatality is almost expected with this training. A second is tough but not a surprise. However, when a third goes missing? It's hard to not be suspicious. When the missing man is connected to one of the elite Maverick team members and is a special friend of Lieutenant Commander Mason Callister? All hell breaks loose …

LIEUTENANT COMMANDER MASON Callister walked into the private office and stood in front of retired Navy Commander Doran Magellan.

"Mason, good to see you."

Yet the dry tone of voice, and the scowl pinching the silver-haired man, all belied his words. Mason had known Doran for over a decade, and their friendship had only grown over time.

Mason waited, as he watched the other man try to work the new tech phone system on his desk. With his hand circling the air above the black box, he appeared to hit buttons randomly.

Mason held back his amusement but to no avail.

"Why can't a phone be a phone anymore?" the commander snapped, as his glare shifted from Mason to the box and back.

Asking the commander if he needed help wouldn't make the older man feel any better, but sitting here and watching as he indiscriminately punched buttons was a struggle. "Is Helen away?" Mason asked.

"Yes, damn it. She's at lunch, and I need her to be at lunch." The commander's piercing gaze pinned Mason in place. "No one is to know you're here."

Solemn, Mason nodded. "Understood."

"Doran? Is that you?" A crotchety voice slammed into the room through the phone's speakers. "Get away from that damn phone. You keep clicking buttons in my ear. Get

Helen in there to do this."

"No, she can't be here for this."

Silence came first, then a huge groan. "Damn it. Then you should have connected me last, so I don't have to sit here and listen to you fumbling around."

"Go pour yourself a damn drink then," Doran barked. "I'm working on the others."

A snort was his only response.

Mason bit the inside of his lip, as he really tried to hold back his grin. The retired commander had been hell on wheels while on active duty, and, even now, the retired part of his life seemed to be more of a euphemism than anything.

"Damn things …"

Mason looked around the dark mahogany office and the walls filled with photos, awards, medals. A life of purpose, accomplishment. And all of that had only piqued his interest during the initial call he'd received, telling him to be here at this time.

"Ah, got it."

Mason's eyebrows barely twitched, as the commander gave him a feral grin. "I'd rather lead a warship into battle than deal with some of today's technology."

As he was one of only a few commanders who'd been in a position to do such a thing, it said much about his capabilities.

And much about current technology.

The commander leaned back in his massive chair and motioned to the cart beside Mason. "Pour three cups."

Interesting. Mason walked a couple steps across the rich tapestry-style carpet and lifted the silver service to pour coffee into three very down-to-earth-looking mugs.

"Black for me."

Mason picked up two cups and walked one over to Doran.

"Thanks." He leaned forward and snapped into the phone, "Everyone here?"

Multiple voices responded.

Curiouser and curiouser. Mason recognized several of the voices. Other relics of an era gone by. Although not a one would like to hear that, and, in good faith, it wasn't fair. Mason had thought each of these men were retired, had relinquished power. Yet, as he studied Doran in front of him, Mason had to wonder if any of them actually had passed the baton or if they'd only slid into the shadows. Was this planned with the government's authority? Or were these retirees a shadow group to the government?

The tangible sense of power and control oozed from Doran's words, tone, stature—his very pores. This man might be heading into his sunset years—based on a simple calculation of chronological years spent on the planet—but he was a long way from being out of the action.

"Mason …" Doran began.

"Sir?"

"We've got a problem."

Mason narrowed his gaze and waited.

Doran's glare was hard, steely hard, with an icy glint. "Do you know the Mavericks?"

Mason's eyebrows shot up. The black ops division was one of those well-kept secrets, so, therefore, everyone knew about it. He gave a decisive nod. "I do."

"And you're involved in the logistics behind the ICE training program in the Arctic, are you not?"

"I am." Now where was the commander going with this?

"Do you know another SEAL by the name of Mountain

Rode? He's been working for the black ops Mavericks." At his own words, the commander shook his head. "What the hell was his mother thinking when she gave him that moniker?"

"She wasn't thinking anything," said the man with a hard voice from behind Mason.

He stiffened slightly, then relaxed as he recognized that voice too.

"She died giving birth to me. And my full legal name is Mountain Bear Rode. It was my father's doing."

The commander glared at the new arrival. "Did I say you could come in?"

"Yes." Mountain's voice was firm, yet a definitive note of affection filled his tone.

That emotion told Mason so much.

The commander harrumphed, then cleared his throat. "Mason, we're picking up a significant amount of chatter over that ICE training. Most of it good. Some of it the usual caterwauling we've come to expect every time we participate in a joint training mission. This one is set to run for six months, then to reassess."

Mason already knew this. But he waited for the commander to get around to why Mason was here, and, more important, what any of this had to do with the mountain of a man who now towered beside him.

The commander shifted his gaze to Mountain, but he remained silent.

Mason noted Mountain was not only physically big but damn imposing and severely pissed, seemingly barely holding back the forces within. His body language seemed to yell, *And the world will fix this, or I'll find the reason why.*

For a moment Mason felt sorry for the world.

Finally a voice spoke through the phone. "Mason, this is Alpha here. I run the Mavericks. We've got a problem with that ICE training center. Mountain, tell him."

Mason shifted to include Mountain in his field of vision. Mason wished the other men on the conference call were in the room too. It was one thing to deal with men you knew and could take the measure of; it was another when they were silent shadows in the background.

"My brother is one of the men who reported for the Artic training three weeks ago."

"Tergan Rode?" Mason confirmed. "I'm the one who arranged for him to go up there. He's a great kid."

A glimmer of a smile cracked Mountain's stony features. He nodded. "Indeed. A bright light in my often dark world. He's a dozen years younger than me, just passed his BUD/s training this spring, and raring to go. Until his raring to go then got up and went."

Oh, shit. Mason's gaze zinged to the commander, who had kicked up his feet to rest atop the big desk. Stocking feet. With Mickey Mouse images dancing on them. Sidetracked, Mason struggled to pull his attention back to Mountain. "Meaning?"

"He's disappeared." Mountain let out a harsh breath, as if just saying that out loud, and maybe to the right people, could allow him to relax—at least a little.

The commander spoke up. "We need your help, Mason. You're uniquely qualified for this problem."

It didn't sound like he was qualified in any way for anything he'd heard so far. "Clarify." His spoken word was simplicity itself, but the tone behind it said he wanted the cards on the table … now.

Mountain spoke up. "He's the third incident."

Mason's gaze narrowed, as the reports from the training

camp rolled through his mind. "One was Russian. One was from the German SEAL team. Both were deemed accidental deaths."

"No, they weren't."

There it was. The root of the problem in black-and-white. He studied Mountain, aiming for neutrality. "Do you have evidence?"

"My brother did."

"Ah, hell."

Mountain gave a clipped nod. "I'm going to find him."

"Of that I have no doubt," Mason said quietly. "Do you have a copy of the evidence he collected?"

"I have some of it." Mountain held out a USB key. "This is your copy. Top secret."

"We don't have to remind you, Mason, that lives are at stake," Doran added. "Nor do we need another international incident. Consider also that a group of scientists, studying global warming, is close by, and not too far away is a village home to a few hardy locals."

Mason accepted the key, turned to the commander, and asked, "Do we know if this is internal or enemy warfare?"

"We don't know at this point," Alpha replied through the phone. "Mountain will lead Shadow Recon. His mission is twofold. One, find out what's behind these so-called accidents and put a stop to it by any means necessary. Two, locate his brother, hopefully alive."

"And where do I come in?" Mason asked.

"We want you to pull together a special team. The members of Shadow Recon will report to both you and Mountain, just in case."

That was clear enough.

"You'll stay stateside but in constant communication with Mountain—with the caveat that, if necessary, you're on the next flight out."

"What about bringing in other members from the Mavericks?" Mason suggested.

Alpha took this question too, his response coming through via Speakerphone. "We don't have the numbers. The budget for our division has been cut. So we called the commander to pull some strings."

That was Doran's cue to explain further. "Mountain has fought hard to get me on board with this plan, and I'm here now. The navy has a special budget for Shadow Recon and will take care of Mountain and you, Mason, and the team you provide."

"Skills needed?"

"Everything," Mountain said, his voice harsh. "But the biggest is these men need to operate in the shadows, mostly alone, without a team beside them. Too many new arrivals will alert the enemy. If we make any changes to the training program, it will raise alarms. We'll move the men in one or two at a time on the same rotation that the trainees are running right now."

"And when we get to the bottom of this?" Mason looked from the commander back to Mountain.

"Then the training can resume as usual," Doran stated.

Mason immediately churned through the names already popping up in his mind. How much could he tell his men? Obviously not much. Hell, he didn't know much himself. How much time did he have? "Timeline?"

The commander's final word told him of the urgency. "Yesterday."

Find Magnus here!

To find out more visit Dale Mayer's website.

https://geni.us/DMSRMagnusUniversal

Author's Note

Thank you for reading Rick's Road: Terkel's Team, Book 5! If you enjoyed the book, please take a moment and leave a short review.

Dear reader,

I love to hear from readers, and you can contact me at my website: www.dalemayer.com or at my Facebook author page. To be informed of new releases and special offers, sign up for my newsletter or follow me on BookBub. And if you are interested in joining Dale Mayer's Reader Group, here is the Facebook sign up page. http://geni.us/DaleMayerFBGroup

Cheers,
Dale Mayer

Get THREE Free Books Now!

Have you met the SEALS of Honor?

SEALs of Honor Books 1, 2, and 3. Follow the stories of brave, badass warriors who serve their country with honor and love their women to the limits of life and death.

Read Mason, Hawk, and Dane right now for FREE.

Go here and tell me where to send them!
https://dalemayer.com/masonfree

About the Author

Dale Mayer is a *USA Today* best-selling author, best known for her SEALs military romances, her Psychic Visions series, and her Lovely Lethal Garden cozy series. Her contemporary romances are raw and full of passion and emotion (Broken But … Mending, Hathaway House series). Her thrillers will keep you guessing (Kate Morgan, By Death series), and her romantic comedies will keep you giggling (*It's a Dog's Life*, a stand-alone novella; and the Broken Protocols series, starring Charming Marvin, the cat).

Dale honors the stories that come to her—and some of them are crazy, break all the rules and cross multiple genres!

To go with her fiction, she also writes nonfiction in many different fields, with books available on résumé writing, companion gardening, and the US mortgage system. All her books are available in print and ebook format.

Connect with Dale Mayer Online

Dale's Website – www.dalemayer.com
Twitter – @DaleMayer
Facebook Page – geni.us/DaleMayerFBFanPage
Facebook Group – geni.us/DaleMayerFBGroup
BookBub – geni.us/DaleMayerBookbub
Instagram – geni.us/DaleMayerInstagram
Goodreads – geni.us/DaleMayerGoodreads
Newsletter – geni.us/DaleNews

Also by Dale Mayer

Published Adult Books:

Shadow Recon
Magnus, Book 1

Bullard's Battle
Ryland's Reach, Book 1
Cain's Cross, Book 2
Eton's Escape, Book 3
Garret's Gambit, Book 4
Kano's Keep, Book 5
Fallon's Flaw, Book 6
Quinn's Quest, Book 7
Bullard's Beauty, Book 8
Bullard's Best, Book 9
Bullard's Battle, Books 1–2
Bullard's Battle, Books 3–4
Bullard's Battle, Books 5–6
Bullard's Battle, Books 7–8

Terkel's Team
Damon's Deal, Book 1
Wade's War, Book 2
Gage's Goal, Book 3
Calum's Contact, Book 4
Rick's Road, Book 5

Scott's Summit, Book 6

Kate Morgan

Simon Says… Hide, Book 1
Simon Says… Jump, Book 2
Simon Says… Ride, Book 3
Simon Says… Scream, Book 4
Simon Says… Run, Book 5

Hathaway House

Aaron, Book 1
Brock, Book 2
Cole, Book 3
Denton, Book 4
Elliot, Book 5
Finn, Book 6
Gregory, Book 7
Heath, Book 8
Iain, Book 9
Jaden, Book 10
Keith, Book 11
Lance, Book 12
Melissa, Book 13
Nash, Book 14
Owen, Book 15
Percy, Book 16
Quinton, Book 17
Hathaway House, Books 1–3
Hathaway House, Books 4–6
Hathaway House, Books 7–9

The K9 Files

Ethan, Book 1

Pierce, Book 2

Zane, Book 3

Blaze, Book 4

Lucas, Book 5

Parker, Book 6

Carter, Book 7

Weston, Book 8

Greyson, Book 9

Rowan, Book 10

Caleb, Book 11

Kurt, Book 12

Tucker, Book 13

Harley, Book 14

Kyron, Book 15

Jenner, Book 16

Rhys, Book 17

The K9 Files, Books 1–2

The K9 Files, Books 3–4

The K9 Files, Books 5–6

The K9 Files, Books 7–8

The K9 Files, Books 9–10

The K9 Files, Books 11–12

Lovely Lethal Gardens

Arsenic in the Azaleas, Book 1

Bones in the Begonias, Book 2

Corpse in the Carnations, Book 3

Daggers in the Dahlias, Book 4

Evidence in the Echinacea, Book 5

Footprints in the Ferns, Book 6

Gun in the Gardenias, Book 7
Handcuffs in the Heather, Book 8
Ice Pick in the Ivy, Book 9
Jewels in the Juniper, Book 10
Killer in the Kiwis, Book 11
Lifeless in the Lilies, Book 12
Murder in the Marigolds, Book 13
Nabbed in the Nasturtiums, Book 14
Offed in the Orchids, Book 15
Poison in the Pansies, Book 16
Quarry in the Quince, Book 17
Revenge in the Roses, Book 18
Lovely Lethal Gardens, Books 1–2
Lovely Lethal Gardens, Books 3–4
Lovely Lethal Gardens, Books 5–6
Lovely Lethal Gardens, Books 7–8
Lovely Lethal Gardens, Books 9–10

Psychic Vision Series

Tuesday's Child
Hide 'n Go Seek
Maddy's Floor
Garden of Sorrow
Knock Knock…
Rare Find
Eyes to the Soul
Now You See Her
Shattered
Into the Abyss
Seeds of Malice
Eye of the Falcon
Itsy-Bitsy Spider

Unmasked

Deep Beneath

From the Ashes

Stroke of Death

Ice Maiden

Snap, Crackle…

What If…

Talking Bones

String of Tears

Psychic Visions Books 1–3

Psychic Visions Books 4–6

Psychic Visions Books 7–9

By Death Series

Touched by Death

Haunted by Death

Chilled by Death

By Death Books 1–3

Broken Protocols – Romantic Comedy Series

Cat's Meow

Cat's Pajamas

Cat's Cradle

Cat's Claus

Broken Protocols 1-4

Broken and… Mending

Skin

Scars

Scales (of Justice)

Broken but… Mending 1-3

Glory

Genesis

Tori

Celeste

Glory Trilogy

Biker Blues

Morgan: Biker Blues, Volume 1

Cash: Biker Blues, Volume 2

SEALs of Honor

Mason: SEALs of Honor, Book 1

Hawk: SEALs of Honor, Book 2

Dane: SEALs of Honor, Book 3

Swede: SEALs of Honor, Book 4

Shadow: SEALs of Honor, Book 5

Cooper: SEALs of Honor, Book 6

Markus: SEALs of Honor, Book 7

Evan: SEALs of Honor, Book 8

Mason's Wish: SEALs of Honor, Book 9

Chase: SEALs of Honor, Book 10

Brett: SEALs of Honor, Book 11

Devlin: SEALs of Honor, Book 12

Easton: SEALs of Honor, Book 13

Ryder: SEALs of Honor, Book 14

Macklin: SEALs of Honor, Book 15

Corey: SEALs of Honor, Book 16

Warrick: SEALs of Honor, Book 17

Tanner: SEALs of Honor, Book 18

Jackson: SEALs of Honor, Book 19

Kanen: SEALs of Honor, Book 20

Nelson: SEALs of Honor, Book 21

Taylor: SEALs of Honor, Book 22
Colton: SEALs of Honor, Book 23
Troy: SEALs of Honor, Book 24
Axel: SEALs of Honor, Book 25
Baylor: SEALs of Honor, Book 26
Hudson: SEALs of Honor, Book 27
Lachlan: SEALs of Honor, Book 28
Paxton: SEALs of Honor, Book 29
SEALs of Honor, Books 1–3
SEALs of Honor, Books 4–6
SEALs of Honor, Books 7–10
SEALs of Honor, Books 11–13
SEALs of Honor, Books 14–16
SEALs of Honor, Books 17–19
SEALs of Honor, Books 20–22
SEALs of Honor, Books 23–25

Heroes for Hire

Levi's Legend: Heroes for Hire, Book 1
Stone's Surrender: Heroes for Hire, Book 2
Merk's Mistake: Heroes for Hire, Book 3
Rhodes's Reward: Heroes for Hire, Book 4
Flynn's Firecracker: Heroes for Hire, Book 5
Logan's Light: Heroes for Hire, Book 6
Harrison's Heart: Heroes for Hire, Book 7
Saul's Sweetheart: Heroes for Hire, Book 8
Dakota's Delight: Heroes for Hire, Book 9
Tyson's Treasure: Heroes for Hire, Book 10
Jace's Jewel: Heroes for Hire, Book 11
Rory's Rose: Heroes for Hire, Book 12
Brandon's Bliss: Heroes for Hire, Book 13
Liam's Lily: Heroes for Hire, Book 14

SEALs of Steel

SEALs of Steel, Books 1–8

The Mavericks

Kerrick, Book 1
Griffin, Book 2
Jax, Book 3
Beau, Book 4
Asher, Book 5
Ryker, Book 6
Miles, Book 7
Nico, Book 8
Keane, Book 9
Lennox, Book 10
Gavin, Book 11
Shane, Book 12
Diesel, Book 13
Jerricho, Book 14
Killian, Book 15
Hatch, Book 16
Corbin, Book 17
Aiden, Book 18
The Mavericks, Books 1–2
The Mavericks, Books 3–4
The Mavericks, Books 5–6
The Mavericks, Books 7–8
The Mavericks, Books 9–10
The Mavericks, Books 11–12

Collections

Dare to Be You…
Dare to Love…
Dare to be Strong…

RomanceX3

Standalone Novellas

It's a Dog's Life
Riana's Revenge
Second Chances

Published Young Adult Books:

Family Blood Ties Series

Vampire in Denial
Vampire in Distress
Vampire in Design
Vampire in Deceit
Vampire in Defiance
Vampire in Conflict
Vampire in Chaos
Vampire in Crisis
Vampire in Control
Vampire in Charge
Family Blood Ties Set 1–3
Family Blood Ties Set 1–5
Family Blood Ties Set 4–6
Family Blood Ties Set 7–9
Sian's Solution, A Family Blood Ties Series Prequel
    Novelette

Design series

Dangerous Designs
Deadly Designs
Darkest Designs
Design Series Trilogy

Standalone
In Cassie's Corner
Gem Stone (a Gemma Stone Mystery)
Time Thieves

Published Non-Fiction Books:

Career Essentials
Career Essentials: The Résumé
Career Essentials: The Cover Letter
Career Essentials: The Interview
Career Essentials: 3 in 1